Flushed

J.J. Zbylski

Clean Reads
ALL STORY. NO GUILT.
www.CleanReads.com

By observing I've learned to be an observer.
By daydreaming I've learned to be a daydreamer.
Similarly I've become a thinker, a ponderer, a tinkerer, and a wanderer.

By being a daughter I've learned to be a mom.
And by having tried-and-true friends I've learned to be one.
I've trained to be a student, a pharmacist, an employee.
I'm even studying to become a proper pirate. Huzzah!

I've taught myself to take a chance, put myself out there, and give it a shot.
I've learned not to fear opportunity, but to fear the undone.

There have been many teachers in my life and I thank them all.

But this book is for my very first teacher.

The one who taught me how to learn.
My mom.

Chapter One

⚓

Lucas sat at his tiny school desk, trying desperately to focus on the exam and not his digestion. The greasy hair-netted lunch lady had sabotaged him. Who served double-bean burritos before silent test-taking time? The only thing worse would be double-bean burritos directly before PE-class partnered sit-ups.

His stomach gurgled, and he felt air moving down his intestines. It was only a matter of time before he burst. And in this silent classroom of test-takers, it would be embarrassing. Lucas mentally shrugged. When was he ever embarrassed of passing gas? Burping? Never.

Why would he care? He was nearly twelve years old. His buddies burped more than he did. He didn't care what girls thought. He was the perfect age to appreciate his mud-wallowing, belch-issuing, turd-producing body. After all, everybody had bodily functions. And these were about to blast him to the moon any second.

Whatever moved through Lucas's insides made him squirm. He looked to the left and saw red-headed Tabitha, oblivious to his discomfort. To the other side was Chuck, a baseball buddy. He knew what was up, since the baseball guys ate burritos together at lunch. Lucas crossed his legs and bit his lip while Chuck mimed a laugh.

He clenched his butt-cheeks together, attempting to finish his math test before exploding. He finished up the last question, double-checked it... It was a habit engrained in him, and most of the world, to suppress nature. Silence your toots. Cover your burps. Say excuse me.

Nature had its own piece to say about it. And at the moment, its voice sounded like a gurgling juicy toot. *Frraaapp.* The silent room seemed even more silent in the wake of his noisy outburst. Time stopped.

Lucas wondered whether to look around proudly to see who'd heard him, or if he should carry on like nothing had ever happened. He smirked, let his pride get the best of him, and looked around the room at the wide-eyed horrified faces of his classmates.

Elderly Mrs. Anthony barely raised her eyes from her desk as she spoke.

"Excuse yourself, Lucas."

"Why? It's nature."

"It's polite, Lucas. Class, carry on with your exam. Time has not stopped for this disruption. Excuse yourself and continue with your exam, Lucas." Mrs. Anthony let her glasses slide down her nose and gave Lucas a look over the frames.

A rebellious streak fired up in Lucas. He was done with his math test anyway. Math was easy. Holding in gas was not easy. He knew what he was going to do before his body caught up with his plans of destruction. After all, it was only natural. He paused, calibrating... *poooooot.*

"Excuse me!" Lucas hollered right as his rump sounded its own fanfare.

"Thank you, I think." Mrs. Anthony looked back down at her desk.

Chuck laughed aloud and reached out to slap Lucas a five. Lucas fist-bumped his buddy and smirked at Tabitha who hid behind her hoodie sleeve.

"Go to the toilet before you explode." Tabitha choked behind her sleeve.

"Good idea." Lucas smiled at her.

Lucas knew Tabitha a little bit, since they'd partnered up for a class project last quarter. He'd gone to her grandmother's house where Tabitha lived. The grandmother had been pretty nice, despite her loose dentures and smelling like... well, a smelling like a grandmother. He wasn't sure why she lived with her grandma instead of her mom or dad, but she wouldn't tell him. He'd asked her once while procrastinating on their project, but she'd ignored him completely. It had been a sore point for her, so Lucas had let it slide. They weren't exactly friends, but not exactly enemies. Tabitha was kinda mean, but not toward anyone in particular. Frenemies, Lucas figured, if that word was even a real thing.

"Can I go to the bathroom?" Lucas asked.

"Lucas, I am attempting to ignore your embarrassingly noisy bodily functions, but please stop talking during the exam," Mrs. Anthony said.

"It's an emergency. Please please *please please...*" Lucas said.

"Lucas, this could have been handled much better by quietly coming to my desk. Come here and get your detention slip." Mrs. Anthony ripped off a pink slip of paper and scratched on it with her pencil.

The class made obnoxious *oohh* noises. Lucas wound up for a rebuttal.

"This is unfair. Totally unfair. You can't give me detention for what the lunch lady did to me. I've been poisoned. Poisoned with double-bean burritos!" Lucas pulled his hair with exasperation.

"Maybe the lunch lady also affected your hearing. You're not being given detention for passing gas. You're being given detention for interrupting the exam for the entire class instead of just yourself." Mrs. Anthony waved the pink slip of paper.

Lucas stood and marched to the front for his detention slip. Tabitha gave him a helpless shrug, and Chuck looked away. Lucas turned in his completed exam, resigned to his fate. He slouched and frowned at Mrs. Anthony.

"Lucas..." Mrs. Anthony beckoned him for a private word.

"What?" Lucas was impatient; his intestines were gurgling again.

"Here's the bathroom pass too, in case all that noise is the double-bean burrito screaming to get out." Mrs. Anthony hid a smile.

Lucas took it and zipped out the door.

Lucas took his sweet time in the bathroom. All that showed up was air, but he did his part to keep the peace in class by letting it out alone in a stall. *Pooot... oot... oot...* it echoed through the empty bathroom.

After a few minutes, staring at the bathroom's graffiti got boring. Nothing was happening, and the toilet seat was branding itself into his hiney.

"Anybody in there?" A voice echoed in the tiled bathroom. Heavy footsteps clunked around.

"Yeah..." Lucas wondered what was up. The voice was familiar, but the echoes threw him off.

"I'm the plumber. I'm setting up."

Lucas realized why the voice sounded familiar. Dad was a plumber. Dad was at school?

"Dad?" Lucas said.

"Lucas? My little Dingleberry. What a crazy random happenstance," Dad said.

Lucas groaned. Dad was a nerd and always said nerdy things. Embarrassing things. Like calling his son Dingleberry. It was funny five years ago, but now it was horrible. Dad had gotten into plumbing because his idol had been that plumber from the dorky old video games. Lucas was into more normal stuff like sports. Baseball, softball, anything that involved hitting stuff with sticks. Video games with guns were okay too, anything besides mutated mushroom soldiers and plumbers.

He finished on the toilet and tried the flusher. It was limp like a wet noodle. Lucas jostled it a couple more times. No flushing. Oh well. Lucas burst out of the stall, and the door banged against the wall behind him. Dad was there in full plumber glory, bent over his toolbox with too much skin showing above his belt.

"Dad…" Lucas groaned and covered his eyes.

"Don't tell me you were in the out-of-order stall." Dad got up with a grunt and let his head fall back with frustration. He wore his embarrassing plumber uniform. The shirt was an old-fashioned bowling outfit that said his name, Carl, and the plumbing company's name, Viking Plumbers. His head was topped off with a trucker hat with foam horns on the sides. Lucas saw the uniform plenty, but he still laughed in his dad's face. It was that pathetic.

"The what?" Lucas looked back at the stall he used. The door still swung back and forth. There was a junky little sign that read *Out-of-Order*. He rolled his eyes. Someone had failed at sign-making. Those who need to go needed flashing neon to distract them from their mission.

"Oh."

"You better not have gone number-two in there without flushing."

"If I did, it was only 'cause the plumbing's broken. When have I ever forgotten to flush?" Lucas laughed. He had about a fifty-percent success rate when it came to flushing.

"Very funny. You'll be sorry when sewer pirates come to get you," Dad said.

"Dad. *Daaaad*. Not at school, Dad," Lucas said. At least he called them sewer pirates today. Lucas had heard everything from *privyteers* to *buttcaneers* from Dad. Totally groan-worthy humor.

Lucas edged toward the door. Dad was so thoroughly embarrassing he thought he would die from it. The school setting increased the embarrassment factor.

"It's true. If you don't flush after yourself, they'll come up through the sewers and drag you away. Down into the sewers. Where this dirty old bathroom looks like a palace in comparison. Believe me, I'm a plumber. I've seen what's creeping around down there in the dark of the sewers. Alligators… Rats bigger than Labradors… Lots of other things I don't even have names for. But worst of all, most worstest of all, are the pirates," Dad lectured.

Lucas heard this all before and didn't give it an ounce of credit. He waved at his dorky dad and bolted out to return his bathroom pass.

"You didn't wash your hands," Dad's voice echoed behind him.

Chapter Two

Lucas came home and camped out in the bathroom to recover from the insanity at school. It was worse than usual today, considering detention and Dad lecturing him. Not only was Dad at school, a considerably bad scenario, but he'd blabbed on and on about some fairytale pirates in the sewers. *Insanity.*

Lucas snapped out of his thoughts with the sound of Mom's hollering. Her voice pierced right through the door. He'd invest in a soundproof and smell-proof door for his bathroom when he became rich and famous.

"What are you doing in there, Lucas? We waited for you to get through with detention, and now you've holed up in the bathroom? Dinner is getting cold. I need enough time to exercise after dinner," Mom yelled.

"Hang on, I'm unloading the groceries," Lucas yelled back. His voice resonated against the walls.

He scrunched his face up and wiped twice, just to make sure.

"Could you please say something from time to time that isn't horribly foul?" Mom yelled.

Lucas frowned. He thought that was a pretty tame way to talk about what went on in the bathroom. Weren't there any girls in the world who were also horribly foul? Maybe that's when he would decide girls were interesting. When one burped at him and didn't excuse herself afterward. He couldn't imagine Mom or the fluorescent-orange-haired Tabitha ever doing that.

Anyway, Lucas wasn't trying to waste time. He wanted to eat as much as anyone in the family. Especially since his entire digestive tract was now ready for more. Poisonous lunch lady! He needed some real nourishment, not beany toxic waste. He would attack his dinner plate, and empty it like his freshly evacuated bowels.

Lucas didn't bother washing his hands or flushing. He dared the sewer-sailing, privy-plundering pirates to come after him. But they wouldn't, since they didn't exist.

It took Lucas an instant to sprint across the house and sit down at the table. He grabbed his fork and dug into the plate before he even knew what had been served. It was some random meat with some random sauce, with something resembling a potato on the side. The usual. Mom brought in some bread from the kitchen while Dad and Lucas's little sister Chelsea sat down.

Dad loved to eat just as much as Lucas. Lucas peeked up at him while chewing. He was still dressed in his dorky work uniform. That couldn't be sanitary. He looked the complete opposite of a Viking, despite the label on his shirt. He'd removed his hat since he'd thought it was polite, but it had exposed his gaping bald spot. Lucas couldn't decide which was worse. Both versions of his head were mortifying.

Mom was a slender woman, who tended to cook more than she ate, and exercised off any clinging calories. Lucas thought she was a twitchy grump, but Chelsea thought she was the best mom on the planet.

Chelsea was seven years old. Lucas figured she still had a few years to become cool. Currently, she drove him completely insane. He wouldn't let anyone else be mean to her, but it was his duty as her big brother to make sure she had her fair share of torture. The sibling discontent was mutual, since Chelsea thought her brother was completely disgusting. That seemed to be the trend among girls, regarding Lucas.

"Did everybody wash their hands?" Mom asked, setting down the bread platter on the table.

"Yes." Lucas lied with his mouth full, halfway through his dinner plate already.

"No," Chelsea said. Frustration dripped from her voice as she climbed down from the chair and scampered across the house to the bathroom.

"So, Lucas, why don't you tell us why you were given detention today," Mom said.

"For farting in class," Lucas said.

"Surely that's not the entire story. Otherwise I'd have been in detention every day from kindergarten to graduation." Dad laughed heartily.

Lucas gave Dad a high five.

"Show us your detention slip." Mom had a grumpy look, but at least it was aimed at Dad just as much as Lucas.

"It's all the way over there…" Lucas complained.

"Tell us what it says, and we'll make you prove it later," Dad said.

"It might say… for talking during the exam?" Lucas suggested.

"Oh well, that's a reasonable complaint," Dad said.

"*Dad*. It wasn't my fault. I was provoked," Lucas said. Dad was supposed to be on his side.

"Surely nobody had a gun to your head, forcing you to speak?" Mom said.

"Obviously," Lucas said.

"Well then, seems like you had it coming," Dad said.

"You just don't understand. I farted really loud, but it wasn't my fault. The lunch lady served double-bean burritos right before the math test. How can I compete with that?" Lucas tried to play the sympathy card.

"So, your rump was talking during the exam, not you?" Mom asked.

"Uh…" Lucas scrambled for a retort.

"Thought not," Mom said.

"Go to the bathroom before the really big ones launch," Dad said.

"I guess. Hey—why are you still dressed up in your dorky outfit anyway? Did you fix the toilet at school?" Lucas tried to change the subject.

"I'm on the swing shift today. This is my lunch break. And yes, I fixed it, no thanks to you," Dad said.

"I didn't even poop in it. It's not my fault. And what did you say? You gotta go back to work? That sucks," Lucas said.

Mom gasped. Dad shrugged. Mom always over-reacted.

"Stop being so rude," Mom said.

Girlish shrieks sounded from the direction of the bathroom.

"*Sick*." Chelsea whined and ran back into the room, "There is doodie in the toilet!"

"Then don't wash your hands in the toilet," Lucas shot back at her. He carried on eating.

Dad shot him a purposeful look. Lucas tried to ignore it and kept eating. He really hoped Dad wasn't going to spout some bathroom-pirate nonsense right here over dinner.

Lucas belched loudly and derailed the whining and the shooting of looks across the table. His lips flapped, and a few soggy crumbs splattered across the table. Dad laughed aloud. He covered his mouth with his napkin and faked coughing into it, but it was too late.

"Carl!" Mom said, shocked. He was not supposed to encourage such behaviors, especially at the dinner table.

"Yes, dear?" Dad said in his embarrassing voice that made Mom act all silly. Despite being a middle-aged balding man, he could still be cute when he tried, according to Mom. Plain gross, according to Lucas.

"Uh... never mind." Mom sighed and sat down at the table, postponing the poop predicament till after dinner.

Chelsea stomped her feet in annoyance and retook her seat. She started eating dinner with her hands as her fork lay forgotten alongside the plate. She picked apart her meat with careful, tiny fingers. She was soon covered with sticky goo that used to be mashed potatoes up to her elbows.

"Oh dear, you didn't wash your hands, did you?" Mom asked.

"No," Chelsea said as she licked her fingers.

Lucas laughed aloud and leaned back in his chair. He clasped his hands over his full belly. He was always the first to finish eating. Dad was wrapping up the feast as well when the tell-tale sound of passing gas ripped through the air. *Frraaapp.* Blameful glances shot toward Lucas. He looked bewildered. For once, his butt cannon hadn't exploded.

"What?" Lucas cried out. His hands flew up in a gesture of innocence.

Poooot. The sound broke loose again, and the culprit was pinpointed. Dad's body posed guiltily in his fart maneuver, leaning to one side on his chair. One of his cheeks was elevated on a cushion of air. Mom rolled her eyes and pushed her plate away, appetite lost. She stood and started to clear away the dishes. Dad kept his mouth shut, wisely. He got up and assisted the table's clearance. Lucas snorted in an attempt to hide his laughter. Chelsea giggled and followed Mom into the kitchen.

Dad and Lucas found themselves alone in the dining room for a moment. Dad gave Lucas a serious look. Lucas smirked. It was tough to take Dad seriously directly after he'd launched a huge fart.

"Seriously, Lucas, don't invite trouble. Flush the toilet. If you don't… They *will* come for you," Dad said.

Dad's eyes were dark, and he wasn't smiling. Lucas wasn't sure how he got stuck with such weird parents. But weirdness aside, Dad's warning was edged with real danger. Lucas forced himself to laugh, but underneath he wasn't sure if it was funny anymore.

Several minutes passed before Mom remembered the dinner drama and hollered across the house at Lucas. Dad took off for the second half of his shift plumbing, plumbering, or whatever it was called. Cleaning up brown gunk, probably. Lucas perched on the couch in front of a glowing television screen. He smacked his forehead with annoyance when the hollering Momster summoned him.

"Lucas… Did you flush the toilet yet? I want you to clean it with this, too." Mom thrust a spray bottle of bathroom disinfectant into Lucas's hand as he lethargically responded to her call.

He stared at it like it was radioactive. She gave him a toilet brush to complete the job. Then she crossed her arms and waited for him to move. Lucas gingerly took the brush, delicately by the handle as if it was a sharp knife. It wasn't sharp, but thoroughly disturbing. It was growing some black goo along the white plastic stick and had some gnarly hairs wound up in the wiry plastic bristles.

"Mom…" Lucas stretched out her title into a whine.

She grabbed her son's shoulders and steered him toward the bathroom door. He resisted, yanking his shoulders out of her hands one at a time, but was easily re-grabbed. They arrived outside the bathroom door. It was open only a crack and dark inside. That was their family's code for it being vacant, without letting too much stink escape.

"Go on, Dingleberry." Mom grinned.

Oh no she didn't. Lucas suffered Dad using that obnoxious nickname but not Mom, too. He took in a deep breath, preparing to yell something foul but got distracted by his sister appearing on scene.

"Hurry up. I have to go potty," Chelsea whined.

"It's called pee, not potty," Lucas argued. He poked the toilet brush in Chelsea's direction. She dodged and squealed.

"Potty." Chelsea said again.

"Unless you mean poop. Is that what you gotta do? You know, make some turds, floaters, chunks, feces, poo-poo—"

Mom looked horrified at his dirty mouth, but Lucas thought he saw a little pride for his wide vocabulary in there too. Either way, she gave up the fight and went into her room to change into her Latin dance wardrobe. It was almost time for her noisy aerobics.

"You're disgusting," Chelsea complained to Lucas.

"I know. That's not even the first time I heard that today." Lucas laughed.

"Let me go first," she begged. She apparently forgot that the toilet was filled with poo.

"No," Lucas said.

He didn't even care whether she went first, but it was in his nature to argue with her. His duty as a big brother, really. He nudged her out of the way, slipped through the door, and locked himself in the bathroom. He fumbled for the light switch in the dark with his hands full.

"I gotta go..." Chelsea whined through the door. She banged on it with her tiny fists.

"Wait! Mom says I gotta clean," Lucas yelled through the door.

Lucas started to get annoyed with the lights off. It reeked in the bathroom; he must have done worse than he'd realized in the toilet. He jabbed the wall with his elbow and finally turned on the lights. His funny bone took the hit and stung like crazy. Lucas turned toward the toilet and screamed like a little girl, but not because of his elbow. Lucas was not alone in the bathroom.

Chapter Three

The sight in the bathroom completely perplexed Lucas. He stood there like a statue as the scream died on his lips.

"Stop making fun of me. I don't scream like that. I'm telling Mom!" Chelsea's feet thumped away, down the hallway.

The lower half of someone stuck out from the cabinets under the sink. Whoever it was appeared to be either a vagabond or a dirty carnival performer.

He had dingy brown trousers that may have been red once. They were altogether too baggy and hung off of him like a hastily folded circus tent. He had boots too, monstrously huge black things that flopped over themselves. They may have reached his thighs if not so floppy, but they were wrinkled around his ankles. A battered belt held up the grungy pants. Actually, it was a series of belts working together to hold up a slew of objects. There weren't any belt loops, and the tools dangling from the belts were held more securely than the pants themselves.

The intruder backed up. If Lucas hadn't been terrified, he might have made a beeping noise like he did when trucks moved backward. Lucas watched as the guy's head hit the underside of the sink with a loud thump and growled a roar of a complaint. His big body spilled out onto the rug before he spun around at surprising speed to face Lucas.

"Avast, Dingleberry," he said.

Lucas laughed at him. In fact, he didn't appear to be a hobo at all. He was a smelly old pirate with long hair matted in a mixture of dreadlocks and tangles. The crown of his head was wrapped in a chunk of bath towel as discolored as his trousers. He wore a stained, off-white shirt with puffy sleeves and a V-neck, showing off a big mermaid tattoo on his chest. The worst thing of all was he'd somehow picked up on Lucas's dorky nickname. Mom would pay for this.

"Who are you supposed to be?" Lucas finally found the words to question the intruder.

"Aargh! Let me naked blade be answerin' that there question for ye." The piratey-bum-intruder withdrew something from his belt. The object looked more like a plunger than a sword.

"What's that?" Lucas wasn't threatened by the awkward man with the tangled hair and speech impediment.

"Me cutlass, that be what." Oh yeah, cutlasses. Lucas had heard plenty of pirate words, thanks to recent movies. This looked like something to unclog a toilet, but with a pointy end. The pirate-guy had the nerve to poke the plungery-cutlass in Lucas's general direction. Lucas found his reflexes working faster than his brain, and he whipped the scummy toilet brush out to defend himself. The two implements clunked when they connected, a little like hitting a homerun. Lucas danced away, trying not to get backed into the corner of the small bathroom. The pirate pranced toward him, still swinging his plungerish blade. Lucas surprised them both by successfully parrying a second thrust with the bristly toilet brush. It wasn't exactly baseball, but it was in the same ballpark. Whack it with the stick.

"Yer not bad, Dingleberry. Yer name be not in vain," the pirate said with an amused look on his face. He finally decided to sheath his weapon.

"Uh, thanks. I guess it just comes natural, because I've never done any sword fighting before. But my name's not Dingleberry," Lucas said.

"Come with me, lad, whatever yer name be. We be needin' fresh young recruits like yerself on me ship." The pirate gestured toward the toilet.

"Wait, what?" Lucas snapped to his senses.

"Ye heard me."

"Who are you, why are you in my bathroom, and what are you talking about?" Lucas demanded.

The sound of Latin music flared up in the television room. It was dance time for Mom. Lucas wondered if he would be heard if he screamed for help. He would try his best if this pirate guy turned out to be a creeper.

"Flatus Codswallup, at yer service."

He made an awkward bow, and his long tangled hair fell forward. Lucas stared at him. He wasn't sure if the pirate was old or just weathered. Lucas was halfway between dialing 911 and keeping him as a pet.

Flatus seemed to remember the large lump on his head from the connection with the sink's underside He rubbed it thoughtfully for a second before getting back to work. He turned his back to Lucas and went back down on his knees to rummage through the cabinets once more. He pulled out an economy-sized package of two-ply toilet paper with a look of utter joy across his face.

"Two-ply! Bless me lucky stars," Flatus cried, hugging the huge package like a teddy bear.

"Um—" Lucas started, before giving up. There were simply no words for his confusion.

"Come along, swab. Bring yer pistol and cutlass," Flatus said.

Flatus moved toward Lucas, who cringed as the odor of the pirate invaded his nostrils. Flatus grabbed the cleaning supplies out of his hands and looped the trigger of the cleanser spray bottle through a little strap on the side of Lucas's cargo shorts. Next, he took the dirty, white toilet brush and stuck it through a belt loop on the other side, looking satisfied with himself. Who knew the little strappy things on cargo shorts had function?

Lucas's personal bubble had been invaded. He was in shock. If he'd been anywhere other than his tiny bathroom, he would have dodged. As it stood, he had no escape.

Flatus smiled, and Lucas stared at him. He anticipated a toothless grin for such a poorly groomed pirate, but his teeth were flawless. And Flatus's breath smelled minty fresh—a stark contrast to the rest of his funky-smelling self.

"Have ye any denture glue?" Flatus's grin made way for seriousness.

"Um, no. That must be how you've got perfect teeth, right? They're fake."

Lucas fiddled with his makeshift utility belt. Is this why they're called cargo shorts? To hold cargo? Brilliant.

"Nay! I was born with these ivories. It be in me blood, flawless teeth. Denture glue be the only remedy for the leaky hull of me ship. How about a tongue scraper? That, matey, be the only thing fit for barnacle removal. Me tongue be flawless, as well." Flatus stuck out his tongue for emphasis.

"Sorry—" Lucas found himself oddly apologetic for the lack of things to plunder from his bathroom. He thought for a second, what else would pirates need that his parents wouldn't kill him for handing over?

"Need any shampoo?" Lucas asked.

Flatus laughed so loudly Lucas turned away and closed his eyes. A few flecks of spittle found him anyway.

"Do I look like I be needin' shampoo? Don't mind if I help meself to yer grog though. Come along now, time be a-wastin'." Flatus picked up a half-full bottle of mouthwash.

"But... I don't wanna go with you," Lucas said.

Flatus either didn't believe him or didn't care. The pirate captain hefted Lucas over his shoulder in a fireman's carry, along with the huge pack of toilet paper. Lucas gagged, his face pressed against the dirty pirate's shirt. He didn't think things could get any weirder until Flatus stepped into the toilet. Remnants of Lucas's burritos sloshed around his boots. The smell of feces and unwashed pirate nauseated Lucas, and it tripled when Flatus depressed the lever and flushed them.

Lucas would have shrieked like a little girl if he hadn't been completely underwater. Not just underwater like a swimming pool or a bathtub, but underwater in poo-infested sewer water. Luckily it didn't last long; the drainpipe opened up into more of a waterslide. He reached out and groped about for something to grab on-to but found only questionable gooey chunks. Lucas regretted not flushing and still couldn't believe Dad had been right about the pirates. Inconceivable!

Lucas and Flatus launched out of the pipe and became airborne for an instant before colliding with a wooden surface. Lucas hit his head on the planks hard, but that didn't hurt quite so much as Flatus's huge body landing on his chest and crushing him.

"Cap'n," several voices rang out.

Lucas flailed and tried to shove the smelly pirate off him. Now they were both wet, and Lucas suspected he smelled just as bad as Flatus. His arms were streaked with brown, and he didn't want to know what it was. Don't wanna know. Don't wanna know.

"At ease, lads," Flatus hollered as he rolled off Lucas's body.

The captain reached down and grabbed his hand. Flatus yanked him up so hard Lucas's shoulder hurt and his feet left the planks. From an upright position, Lucas could see he was on some sort of odd boat. A big boat—more like a ship. The main deck was the size of a basketball court, but much scummier.

"Here, ye scurvy swab, take this here and patch that sail." Flatus barked commands at his crew. He shoved the pack of toilet paper in someone's arms.

Lucas watched the crewman grab the plundered TP and take off for the mast. His eyes followed the pirate as he shimmied up the huge pole into the dimness overhead. It wasn't the sky, though. No, it was a dingy black enclosed space. The air was thick with foul mist. Lucas figured this was where farts came to die. If he didn't still feel sick, he would have said the joke aloud.

Looking upward at the sails made Lucas want to fall over backward. The sails were white, the cleanest looking thing around, but not too sturdy. There were jagged tears and loose pieces fluttering in the flatulent breeze. Maybe toilet paper was the best thing to harness such a disgusting wind? Lucas wasn't an expert on sailing in farts—just an expert in their production.

Lucas looked back at the deck and tried to catch his balance. It seemed like things were spinning, but he guessed it was only in his head. His brain was probably still swirling from that epic flush. He knew his stomach was.

The pirate crew bustled around; everyone with a job to do. The crew consisted of some kids, some adults, and even some wrinkly old dudes. They were a ragtag bunch; the only thing they all had in common was being filthy dirty and smelly. Well, the smell could be from the surrounding sewer. Lucas lifted one arm and sniffed his armpit. His gag reflex started up. He choked back a wave of violent nausea. It looked like he had become an official part of the crew, at least as far as body odor was concerned.

"This be our new recruit, Dingleberry," Flatus said.

"Dingleberry," The crew chorused. Some of them dropped their duties and crowded in to see the newbie.

"That's not my name…" Lucas blubbered. He looked around at the pirates seriously, warning them to drop the nickname. He was ready to fight for his naming dignity, sick or not. He wondered if pirates would back down as easily as school bullies had.

"Nay? That be just what they call ye? What be yer true name, lad?" Flatus peered down at Lucas.

"Lucas." As much as he enjoyed wallowing in his own filth, this wasn't exactly what he had in mind.

"Lucas? That be a weak pirate name, swabby. Crewmen, introduce yerselves so Lucas can hear a real pirate name or three," Flatus roared. Someone handed the captain a quintessential pirate hat, and he shoved it on his head right over the towel bandana. It didn't do much to disguise his impressive case of bedhead, but it did help to distinguish him from the hobos and street performers of the world.

"Thumper," said an older dude with one of his feet missing. He had a plunger sucked onto his kneecap and hobbled around awkwardly on its handle.

"Viscous Val. But seriously, Cap'n, this kid looks like a loser. Throw him back," said a zit-faced kid not much older than Lucas. He stared at Lucas as though his eyeballs had laser death rays. Lucas stared right back, and, fortunately, they did not.

"No, you look like a loser," Lucas snapped. Captain Flatus stepped in.

"Belay that talk, Val. Ye will find yerself keel-hauled if this keeps up. Either call him something entertaining like a bilge-sucking butt-barnacle or simply shut it. New recruits mean less duties fer yer scurvy self. And new skills. Mayhaps one day, ye shark bait lot of lubbers will get the *Scumbucket* into tip-top shape. Mayhaps one day, we'll make for open sea. That'll be the day. That'll be the day!" Flatus said.

The pirate captain staggered off, looking inspired. He placed his hand on his mermaid tattoo, roundabouts his heart. Lucas raised an eyebrow and watched him go. The rest of the crew seemed numb to these episodes and kept rattling off their names in introduction.

"Crudd," said a middle-aged career-pirate. His orange dreadlocks were longer than the hair of any girl in Lucas's class. He had a rat perched on his shoulder like a pet parrot.

The introductions droned on. There was Chummy, an old dude with an eye patch and a phlegmy voice and who looked pretty much like his name suggested. There were a few other kids whose clothes ranged all the way from normal to pirate.

Lucas zoned out. There were a bazillion pirates, all equally stinky and all with equally weird names. Lucas was still sore from falling out of a sewer pipe and confused at being flushed down the toilet in the first place. The details went in one ear and out the other.

Some of them wandered off and started working again, while some hung around idly. Maybe searching for a chance to be lazy. A colonially dressed guy in a long, blue brocade coat cut through the hubbub and stood there looking important. Lucas blinked a couple of times, focusing. Why did this guy have so many ruffles on his outfit?

"I am the first mate, Billy Rubin," said the dude. Lucas listened up again, for once. This guy was pretty young but acted older and more serious than even the pirate captain. He walked like there was a stick up his butt. All things considered, he seemed pretty clean and had all his body parts intact, so Lucas humored him.

Billy clip-clopped when he walked because of the shiny black buckled boots he wore. The rest of the crew was basically barefoot. Lucas looked down at his own feet—he'd lost his shoes and one sock. His remaining sock was covered in cold brown water, and he peeled it off, leaving it on the deck. This was nice at least, not having to clean up after himself. He imagined Mom freaking out at a soggy sewer-water infested sock on her floor and smiled.

Flatus swaggered back to where Lucas stood. He gestured and called over some of the crew that had wandered off. Lucas frowned, suspicious of the captain's desire for an audience. Was it time for a public flogging? Or worse, was he going to have his leg sawed off and replaced with a plunger like the big guy? That might make it more difficult to escape. That was the goal of most kidnappers, right? Make their prey immobile? Especially an incompetent ninny like Flatus Codswallup. He needed all the help he could get.

"So what'll we call ye, matey?" Flatus asked.

Lucas tried to answer, but the nausea had made an impressive return, and he grabbed his stomach. Something unsavory gripped his insides, begging to be released. A burp? He opened his mouth wide, expecting the belch to escape. Unfortunately for Billy Rubin, who was the only one fully in the splash zone, Lucas's dinner came up instead. *Hurrrk.*

"Puke," some pirate said.

"State the obvious much?" Lucas choked out.

The first mate turned redder than diaper rash and started to storm off. Flatus grabbed him and pointed him back toward Lucas with a good-natured slap on the back.

"Nay, Billy. It just be a little vomitus. Ye gotta stay put to witness this momenterous occasion. Yer me protégé, me right-hand man, and one day the cap'n proper of the *Scumbucket* here. Consider it baptismal vomit, toughening ye up fer a life of adventure on the seven seas. I'll make a salty dog of yer green hide yet, Mister Rubin," Flatus said.

"I've served you faithfully for a good long time, Captain. Don't devalue me in comparison to this little puke," Billy said.

"Aye, he be Puke," some crewman announced.

"Puke! Puke! Puke! Puke!" the crew chanted, overpowering Billy's complaints.

"Ye got a name, lad. Puke! Though must say I be partial to Dingleberry." Flatus was all smiles.

Lucas burped.

Lucas wasn't sure what was worse, being called Dingleberry or Puke. At least Puke kinda rhymed with his name, and the sound made his head turn. There were some worse names among the crew, so he tried to make the best of it. At least he wasn't named Viscous Val.

The pirates on deck didn't lollygag—Flatus sent them hobbling and hopping off to do their piratey duties. Lucas was left with the first mate Billy Rubin to get acquainted with the ship. After what he had seen of Billy, he wasn't the first choice for a tour guide. And after what Billy had seen of Lucas, the distaste was mutual.

"Here is the location of the captain's cabin," Billy said, pointing.

Lucas wondered why he spoke so fancy-schmancy. The rest of the pirates barely knew English, and here was Billy, proper as the Queen of England. Dad would call it brownnosing. Mom would tell him to relax. Tabitha would probably have a crush on the guy. How did this tidy fool get mixed up with a band of sewer pirates?

Billy cleared his throat and pointed again to the captain's cabin door. Lucas pretended he'd been paying attention all along and examined the door. The entry to Flatus's cabin looked like it had been salvaged from an outhouse. There was a crescent-moon shape carved into the door and the letters W.C.

"What's W.C. stand for?" Lucas asked.

"Where's Captain," Billy said, matter-of-factly.

Lucas thought that was a stupid thing to carve onto a door but didn't think Billy had any better answers hidden up his puffy pirate sleeves. On top of the cabin was another deck, a smaller one with the steering wheel on it. Lucas wanted to check it out.

"Can we go up there?" Lucas asked.

"Yes, Puke, in good time. That is known as the poop deck."

"You've got to bekidding me. The poop deck?" Lucas was on the verge of falling over in a fit of giggles.

"What of it?"

"Poop is like... poop. Feces, doo-doo, chunks, floaters, turds...?" Lucas tried to rustle up some comprehension.

"You are a foul little creature. It's French, *la poupe*."

"Oh." Lucas was not impressed.

"I don't see a future for you in sailing or piracy. You've no respect for authority," Billy said.

Lucas ignored him and walked toward the stairs to the poop deck. He didn't see any future for himself in buttcaneering, either. How could any of them call themselves pirates? They were more like walking, talking turds. When Lucas neared the top of the stairs to the poop deck, he wondered whether anyone had pooped on it as a prank. Then he remembered he was barefoot and instead prayed no one had.

Billy passed him, eager to be the leader of their little tour, and pointed out the helm where the ship was steered. The steering wheel was a toilet seat with some handles sticking out of it to spin it around. There was a good view of the sewer from there. Lucas was surprised how vast the sewers really were. It was dimly lit, but enough light streamed through gutter grates and open manholes to see the massiveness of the underground cavern. Despite the hugeness, it was black and scummy and stinky with earthy smells freely floating through the air. Thick, brown runoff water streamed in from various pipes along the walls. The nausea came back, tickling Lucas's empty stomach.

"Ugh. You guys aren't real pirates. This is insane. Who would want to float around in diarrhea water all day long?" Lucas said.

"Ahem. Some of us are more serious sailors than others, agreed. But Captain Codswallup is sufficiently engineering when it comes to ship repair. As soon as the repairs are completed, we'll see open sea once more. Worry not. And if by chance we shan't see open sea, perhaps a change of leadership is in order..." Billy said.

Lucas thought he was an idiot and no better captain than Flatus. At least Flatus was friendly and didn't mind getting dirty, even if his English was worse. Much worse. Billy wandered off, but Lucas didn't care, so long as he shut up.

In the quiet beyond the first mate's annoying voice, Lucas heard something even more disturbing. Something chomped and snapped alongside the ship's hull. He inched toward the railing and peered over into the ship's shadow to take a closer look. His heart beat faster. He couldn't see anything in the murky dark. He waited, letting his eyes adjust to the gloom. If Dad had been right about his stupid *flushbucklers*, was he also right about the alligators in the sewers? He listened intently. Things became silent.

Then, something smacked him across the back, hard.

Lucas screamed. Captain Flatus laughed and whacked him on the back again, even harder. Lucas scowled. He whirled around and tried to cover up his alarm.

"Ye scream like a girl, Puke."

"Shut up!" Lucas whined. Flatus laughed so hard spittle rained down on him.

"Shut yourself up, Puke. Never talk to the captain like that." Billy reappeared just in time to be obnoxious.

"Precocious lad, eh?" Flatus raised his dirty eyebrows.

Flatus didn't care for Lucas's cheeky retorts. Lucas groaned and shrugged. Despite being much dirtier and more disgusting than home, some things were equally annoying on the sewer pirate ship.

"I'll have none o' yer lip on my ship, Puke. This be the one and only *Scumbucket*. She's seen better days, though, I'll admit. Her hull needs a good patchin'. That be what I want to ask ye," said Flatus.

The pirate captain looped his smelly and dirty arm around Lucas's shoulders, steered him off, and hushed his voice. Lucas leaned in, fighting against the urge to flee his body odor, to hear his words. A couple tiny black fleas jumped out of Flatus's hair onto Lucas's arm. He twitched and shook them off. His stomach rolled again.

"There be only one thing plunderable from bathrooms that'll fix up ol' *Scumbucket*. That be denture glue. Since yer bathroom was despicably free of it, might ye know where to scour?" Flatus looked hopeful.

"Tell your captain where to find the supplies, Puke." Billy squinted at him menacingly.

Lucas stuck out his tongue at Billy and thought for a moment. His grandparents still had their real teeth, plus they lived miles and miles away. The only person he could think of right off the bat who wore dentures was Tabitha's grandmother. He groaned. Of course. The person least likely to handle a bathroom pirate invasion they would invade.

"No. Yes. No." Lucas scratched his arm where the fleas had been.

"Out with it, Puke. Be it an aye or a nay?" Flatus grabbed his shoulders and knelt down, holding him at arm's length.

"Aye? This girl in my class lives with her grandma who wears dentures—" Lucas started but instantly regretted it.

"Billy! Plot a course wherever Puke says," Flatus bellowed and released his grip on Lucas's shoulders.

"Aye-aye, Captain." Billy straightened up in a salute.

"Wait! Can I go home after that?" Lucas scratched his scalp. More fleas? Urgh.

He surprised himself with that request. Was he really so eager to go back to being tidy and polite and bored? It wasn't all toots and giggles down here, though. The snapping thing in the dark caused him some alarm. Lucas was wet and itchy all over, and Billy Rubin was a pain in the butt.

Lucas scratched his rump as he pondered. He could do rude things like rump-scratching anytime in the sewers. But what if Chelsea and Mom started worrying? Called the police? Not that the police could find him down there. They didn't have police cruisers equipped for the sewers. Dad would be pretty disappointed, he was sure of that. He sensed grounding in his future when he returned. If he returned. But worse than any punishment was admitting Dad had been right.

"The Dingleberry wants t'leave us already?" Flatus looked forlorn.

"Shut up. That's not my name. It's Lucas," he said.

"Respect your captain." Billy turned red.

"What, like you do? You're over there plotting to—" Lucas said.

"Shut yer trap, Puke! Set a course, or we'll be dueling. We'll discuss it again after the hull be repaired. Savvy?" Flatus shot him a look.

Lucas shut his trap and crossed his arms. He was caught between failing the captain of his newly discovered pirate crew and being stuck adrift in toilet water for all eternity. Even if they succeeded in patching the ship with denture glue and managed to sail off into the sunset... Billy Rubin would try to overthrow Flatus, and who knew how that'd go down. It seemed like poor Flatus was too dumb to see it. Plus, Lucas wasn't quite ready to admit that he really did care what Tabitha thought of him.

Chapter Four

Flatus shouted a few orders to the crew and herded Lucas into his cabin underneath the poop deck. Lucas couldn't stop smirking every time he heard that term, French or not. Billy was right behind them, harder to shake than a dingleberry.

"Whoa, this is a messed-up office," Lucas said.

Billy Rubin eyeballed him as he prowled around the cabin, but Lucas didn't care. It looked like a lawyer's office mixed with a public restroom stall—how could he not stare at that? He wondered how many households had been plundered to furnish this place.

His bare feet squished on a soft-carpeted floor. Lucas looked down and saw a patchwork of bathroom rugs, some shaped like horseshoes to fit around toilets and some big rectangles to go alongside tubs. A big wooden four-poster bed stood against one wall, fancy in comparison to the rest of the ship. It had plastic shower curtains hanging down for privacy, but one side was slightly ajar. Lucas saw a big, rubber ducky resting next to the pillow. Flatus walked over and shut the curtain. Lucas suppressed a giggle.

Flatus was an aspiring hoarder. The walls held a lot of framed art. Silly and boring art mostly, like in a public restroom. Soothing depictions of tulips and watercolor seascapes weren't too inspiring when he needed to pee. Maybe they were better off plundered into Flatus's collection. Flatus also had a big collection of doohickeys littered about the room with no imaginable purpose. Except maybe the spyglass made out of a toilet paper tube. That could be useful, if it worked.

The wall opposite the bed was full of shelves and cabinets. There were quite a few shelves that had once straddled toilets and an array of medicine cabinets nailed to the wall. Some of the fixtures were pretty fancy. Lucas wondered if any luxury hotels had reported vandalism lately. The shelves held a larger variety than any bathroom Lucas had ever snooped through. Bottles, tubes, and vials held goop that Lucas didn't really want to identify. Ointments, tinctures, liquids, and powders... but apparently no denture glue. There was also a haphazard stack of bathroom-quality literature. Lucas may have cared if he hadn't been living in sewer fantasy world at the moment.

"A seriously messed-up office," Lucas said to himself again. It was messed up, way beyond measure.

"Messed up? Messed up? Nay, lad. This be me throne room. It be anything but messed up!" Flatus yelled.

"It really is a throne room," Lucas said. His eyes caught Flatus's office space.

The room's focal point was a huge wooden desk with a granite countertop. There was a big hole in the middle, probably where a sink had been, but it was plugged up with an oval of wood. Various rolled parchments littered the desk. Behind it sat a fancy porcelain throne. A toilet, actually. Lucas's chin dropped. What he wouldn't give to have a lair like this for his own bathroom. Do his homework while pooping? Heaven. His stomach gurgled. He hadn't seen the last of those bean burritos.

"Do you mind if I... I kinda gotta go—" Lucas headed toward the toilety office chair.

"Avast! Nay, ye scurvy scum. Get yer lumpish larboard side off o' me throne." Flatus stomped around and sat his own rear end onto the toilet before Lucas's rump connected with it, dirty trousers and all.

"Oh, sorry, I thought..."

"You thought wrong, Puke. That is a priceless porcelain throne for a captain's duties, not some reeky chamber pot. Use this, or hang your hindquarters over the railings on deck." Billy harped.

Billy shoved a filthy old bucket into his arms. Lucas dropped it instinctively, gagging. Once he got his senses back, he wished he'd thrown it at Billy instead. That guy was starting to get under his skin. Flatus beckoned them up to the desk. He unrolled a huge piece of drafting paper and spread it out over the desk's surface. A treasure map? After weighting down the curly corners with random junk, he gestured and pointed to things on it. Lucas wasn't bad with maps, so he leaned over and took a look. It wasn't a treasure map after all. It was a diagram of the sewer system.

"This be where we are now, see. This picture be representin' the position o—" Flatus pointed.

"Yeah I know. I can read maps," Lucas said. He was the official navigator of theme parks and other vacation destinations in his family. Once his parents left their hometown, they could get lost in a bathroom stall and never find their way out. Lucas had evolved a sense of direction that had saved them many times.

Lucas checked out the parchment a bit further. It was kinda dull, there weren't any sea monsters doodled in the margins, and there wasn't a proper legend in the corner, but it was informative. The sewer pipes were clearly shown, and the city streets were overlaid, so he knew where they were, despite the yards of earth between them. He recognized Elaine Lane, where he lived. He jabbed it with his finger and moved to the other side of the desk to orient himself. Things fell quickly into place.

"I know this place, it's my street," Lucas said.

"Address the captain properly, you impertinent filth," Billy said.

"Sorry, Captain," Lucas said tentatively. It felt weird. He didn't even speak to Mrs. Anthony as nice as that. Let alone his parents.

"Try this response instead. *Aye-aye, Captain!*" Billy ordered.

"Aye-aye, Captain..." Lucas said. It did have a ring to it. A new sensation pinged him. Maybe he didn't hate the life of a pirate after all.

"Arrgh! That be music to me ears. Maybe yer not such a loggerheaded rogue as I thought," Flatus roared.

The captain stuck his pinky finger into his ear, wiggled it around, and plucked out a chunk of earwax. Lucas scrunched up his nose. He was apparently not as foul himself as he'd once thought. Grossness got much more intense.

"This wayward lad may yet learn to be a part of the crew. If he watches his words," Billy said. He stared daggers at him.

Lucas had read between the lines about Billy's vague threats of displacing the captain. Given the choice between Billy Rubin and Flatus Codswallup, he would pick Flatus time and time again. But he was still holding onto hope of a third choice — going home.

"Who says I want to be a part of this crew?" Lucas said.

Mom would kill him if he hadn't cleaned the toilet and instead had disappeared on a pirate voyage. Either transgression alone would mean being grounded. Both together meant certain death. And whether he wanted to admit it, he'd start missing his family any time now.

"Yer a natural swashbuckler, matey. Ye were born t'be a pirate. Don't talk nonsense. Even yer kin call ye Dingleberry," Flatus insisted.

"That's just a stupid nickname," Lucas said.

No one seemed to believe him or care. Flatus muttered something and focused on the map. Billy stuck his nose in the air.

"But, I can't stay. I have school tomorrow." Lucas tried another tactic.

Why did he care about school? He wasn't sure, but it seemed more important than floating around with turds in the sewers. He was good at schoolwork, when he wasn't being given detention for his bodily functions. He was first to finish that piece-of-cake math test, after all. That was the only reason he wanted to go back, to feel good at stuff. The map reading triggered that feeling of competence, but all in all, this pirate stuff wasn't totally in his comfort zone. Lucas realized the sewer smell wasn't getting to him as much now. Maybe he'd grown used to it – acclimated. A disturbing thought.

"The morrow be a day away. Live in the now, puny matey," Flatus said. He reached over the table and whacked Lucas on the back.

Lucas lurched with the force of the whacking. He shook his head and wondered when his parents would notice he was gone. After Mom got done with her workout video? After Dad got home from work?

At bedtime? After he wasn't in bed to wake up before school? Maybe his parents would be pleasantly surprised it was so quiet and peaceful around the house. Clean, even. Lucas frowned at that thought.

"Stop wallowing in your mangled past life. You say you can read maps, a rare trait among this crew, so prove it. Show us where our required repair material can be found. Point it out now, or I'll swap your hand for a hook," Billy said.

Billy looked at Lucas like he would very much enjoy chopping off his hand. Lucas's fingers fiddled with one another protectively before he pointed out the place where Tabitha lived with her grandma on Marley Boulevard. It was just a few streets over from their current location, the sewer underneath Lucas's house on Elaine Lane. He pointed quickly then jerked his hand back into his damp cargo shorts pocket. He couldn't be too careful. The first mate gave him a nod of approval, but his eyes still looked as though they were daydreaming of ripping off his body parts. Or worse, ripping off his body parts as Billy reigned captain of the *Scumbucket*.

"To the helm!" Captain Flatus yelled.

Lucas got out of the way while the crew changed course. He stood along the railing and watched the thick dark water slosh against the ship's hull. His thoughts got lost again, wondering how he'd ended up as a sewer pirate. Karma, for all the times he'd been snotty to his parents and cheeky to his teacher? Something moved in the water, and Lucas jumped back.

"Jumpy, eh, newbie?" a kid on the crew asked.

"What's down there?" Lucas asked.

"Don't tell me yer afraid of gators," said the kid.

Lucas looked at him. He had blond hair that was dingy with sewer scum. He wore a T-shirt with a popular brand name printed on it but streaked with skid marks. Lucas suddenly didn't care for that brand name anymore. The kid lifted his leg in the air and let out a quick toot, proud as can be. *Pooot.* Lucas decided he needed to speak with his parents about their standards. He had miles to go before becoming disgusting like a drain-dwelling pirate.

"Turbo boost!" The kid cracked himself up pretending the flatulence was propelling him across the deck. Lucas rolled his eyes.

"Wait, are there crocodiles in the sewers?" Lucas heard another chomp in the dark.

"Nope, not a single crocodile in the whole place. Why are you so serious anyway?" The kid looked Lucas up and down. Lucas tried to keep his eyes on his face, not on the streaks on his T-shirt. Lucas held out his arms and let him look. He was annoyed but had nothing to hide.

"Take a picture, it'll last longer," Lucas said.

"What's your name again, newbie?" He ignored the remark.

"Lucas, er, Puke. I guess."

"Oh yeah, Puke. That's a good one. I loved how you spewed all over the deck when the whole crew was watching. Surprised I forgot your name after that. I'm Viscous Val. Not too keen on the name but, who gives a toot. I think when I shook the captain's hand the first time I was sticky. Viscous, Cap'n called it," Val said.

"Hoist the colors," the captain's voice roared over their chatter.

Lucas raised an eyebrow. Val seemed to know what to do and jogged off toward the main mast. Lucas tagged along. Val opened a big basket on deck that looked like a laundry hamper and took out a black towel. Were they stuck on laundry duty now?

"Hold this," Val said.

Lucas obeyed. They stretched out the big black towel, and he saw the white skull image stitched on it. It was almost a traditional Jolly Roger, but instead of crossed bones or swords, they were plungers. They were hoisting the Jolly Plunger.

"Do you know anything about being a pirate? What mast is this?" Val asked.

"The big one?" Lucas guessed.

"Ha! Yes, it's the big one. The one with the crow's nest. It's called the main mast. That one over there toward the back is the mizzenmast." Val talked as he grabbed the rope on the main mast.

Two eyelet holes on the corners of the flag hooked onto a rope on the mast, turning it into a big flagpole. Val hooked the top and let Lucas hook the bottom before hoisting it up. Lucas leaned back to watch it go up toward the crow's nest and got a case of vertigo. The toilet paper sails started to billow, and a rank breeze caught the towel flag as well. Lucas had to look away before he fell over.

"How long have you been here?" Lucas asked Val.

"I dunno. A few days or weeks, I guess. Hard to tell night from day underground," said Val.

"Don't your parents miss you?" Lucas's stomach tingled, but he blamed seasickness over homesickness.

"Don't know, don't care. They complain enough about me they're probably enjoying the vacation. Not sure if I'll ever go back. What for?" said Val.

"Clean clothes and fast-food burgers?" Lucas suggested. He kept the missing his parents bit to himself. He wasn't sure that he even was... yet. Maybe tomorrow.

"Drive-thru takeout? Half the turds down here look more appetizing than a chicken nugget." Val laughed.

Suddenly Val stopped acting like a goofy fool and sniffed the air. Lucas was leery of sniffing around the sewer on purpose, but when the entire crew stopped in their tracks to take a whiff, so did he. It smelled... clean.

"Battle stations! We be under attack!" Captain Flatus's voice rang out across the deck.

"What's going on?" Lucas freaked out, looking around for somewhere to hide or something to grab. Everyone had a job but him.

"Attack, noob. Grab your weapon," Val said.

There was a ruckus as the crew ran back and forth across the deck, arming themselves and battening down the hatches. Tightening the rigging. Hauling up the anchor. All that piratey stuff that Lucas had heard of but couldn't define. He went to stick his hands in his pockets out of uselessness, when he found his weapons. The grimy old toilet brush appeared downright sparkling clean compared to their surroundings, and the bleach solution spray could hopefully have some effect against whatever was attacking.

"What's attacking?" Lucas asked, but Val was gone.

Lucas jogged around through the commotion, looking for somebody whose name he remembered.

The first mate Billy and the captain were up on the poop deck at the helm. Lucas wanted to giggle at the poop deck's name for a second, before realizing how dumb that was. Battle was serious. He climbed the staircase, but his bare feet slipped on mucousy goo as he walked. He grabbed the handrail and pulled himself up the last couple stairs.

"Captain?" Lucas called.

"Not now, Puke, we be busy. Arm yeself, ye tardy-gaited swab," Captain Flatus said.

"But, what's attacking, Captain?"

Lucas got queasy as the boat lurched—they were changing course. Billy was at the helm, wrestling with the toilet-seat steering wheel like his life depended on it. And maybe it did.

"The mortal enemies of this pirate crew, Puke—plumbers." Flatus grabbed the railing hard as the ship's direction was slowly but surely reversed.

"Plumbers? What?" Lucas squeaked.

Lucas hadn't gotten the memo the ship was banking hard to the right, and he lost his footing. His damp bare feet connected with something that might have been a petrified chunk of booger, re-liquefying it and making it a hazard. Lucas's rump connected hard with the deck, reminding him about the bruises he'd gotten earlier after he'd slid out of a sewer pipe. He grabbed a piece of railing and stayed on his butt for the moment, pain and thoughts buzzing around his head.

The mortal enemies of these pirates were plumbers? Like... Dad? Dad didn't seem tough enough to be anything or anyone's enemy, despite having a certain bias against the pirates. Dad couldn't even get the toilets flushed in their household because his threats weren't impressive enough. Lucas frowned. Not only had Dad been right about sewer pirates, there was more to the story.

"Light the lantern, Crudd," Flatus yelled at a passing pirate with long hair.

"Aye-aye, Cap'n," Crudd said, saluting. The fat rat on his shoulder squealed in a salute too.

The pirate had long dreadlocks that swung around him like octopus tentacles as he worked. He had a noisy red-eyed rat on his shoulder that clung to his shirt as he rushed to a contraption that looked halfway between a lighthouse and a metal trashcan. Whatever it was, Crudd set it on fire.

Lucas was firmly planted on his backside as he watched, confused and afraid. The doohickey rotated, blinding Lucas momentarily before it shone out and upward. It was like headlights for the pirate ship.

"We be taking on water, Cap'n," an old phlegmy pirate shouted from mid-ship.

"I know, Chummy, I know. First things first, ye vomit-inducing yeasty louse. We must avoid that villainous poison drain-goo to be avoiding more leaks. The sewer sirens be destructive enough," Flatus yelled.

The lantern's focused light scanned across the grimy cement walls of the sewer as Lucas watched. Cockroaches chattered as they scurried out of the light. Rats stared at them, green eyes reflecting the lantern light back toward the *Scumbucket*. Relatives of the parrot-rat on Crudd's shoulder? Maybe.

Finally the beacon found what it had been looking for, the row of evenly spaced sewer pipes that led up to the houses on this street, like the one Lucas had been flushed down. He rubbed his bruised rump, remembering. The light panned over each in sequence, one after another, after another. They all looked pretty plain, with murky water dripping from them, but nothing to write home about, until —

"Kraken! Kraken ahoy! Off the starboard bow," Billy squealed like a stuck pig.

Lucas shot him a look. Even in the grip of his own cold terror, Lucas wasn't squealing. What a pathetic jerk. As soon as he got the captain on his side, after leading him to the denture glue for repairs, Lucas was going to be the tattletale of all tattletales. He couldn't stomach it if such a creep succeeded in mutiny.

Crudd held the lantern steady on the long skinny thing creeping out of the drain-hole. Wasn't that a plumber's snake like Dad used? It looked like a black garden hose with some nasty pinchers on the end. It grabbed the air with its claspy claw. Toxic green goo poured out around it. The chemically clean scent grew stronger, cutting through the earthy poo smells and making Lucas's eyes sting.

"Cannons at the ready," some pirate yelled from below deck. The sentiment was echoed by several others on the crew.

"Ready starboard cannons. Aim—" Flatus ordered.

The captain marched to mid-ship. He yelled down a big hole in the middle of the deck. He stomped so hard Lucas wondered if he would make the leaky hull even worse. Maybe they'd sink before they ever got to Tabitha's house. He threw up in his mouth a little bit, just imagining swimming through the sewer, and changed his mind. He'd prefer they didn't sink.

"Fire!" Flatus yelled at an inhuman volume. He took off his hat and waved it around for effect. His bed-head was just as impressive as ever.

Flatus's voice echoed off the rounded sewer walls until the earth-shattering crack of cannon fire drowned it out. Bright flashes of light exploded with the booming sound, leaving Lucas's eyes blind and his ears ringing. Was this why he wasn't supposed to blast his music? He went to stick his finger in his ringing ear but stopped, noticing how black it was with sewer slime. His head hurt, and he groaned.

"Hold. Crudd, lantern," Flatus barked.

Cannon smoke blocked the lantern light. The lantern's beam groped around in the smoky darkness as the crew held their breath. The light traced the billowing sulfurous clouds that reeked worse than rotten eggs. Lucas pulled his shirt up over his nose but realized his shirt stank just as bad.

Finally the smoke cleared enough to faintly make out the circular openings to the pipes leading up and out. Lucas thought he saw something twitchy creeping up the shaft. He shivered with the heebie-jeebies. If it was one of those drain-uncloggers Dad used on the job, it sure looked creepier from the sewer side of things.

"Threat neutralized. Break out the grog," Flatus cheered.

"Huzzah!" the ragamuffin crew shouted.

Lucas wasn't sure what grog was, but he had a pretty good guess.

Lucas followed the pour of dirty pirates down the hatch in the middle of the deck to the lower bits of the ship. It was dark down there, but some lanterns that looked like plundered bathroom light fixtures swung on the walls. Instead of bulbs, they'd been refitted with candles. Lucas took the first couple steps downward before realizing the captain and first mate weren't following.

"Cap'n?" Lucas called.

He wasn't sure he wanted to leave his sight. The crew was a bit questionable, Flatus included, but at least he had some authority. Nobody would keelhaul him if he stuck by the captain, right? He also needed to put a bug in Flatus's ear about Billy Rubin's plan. Maybe he was just faking without any intent to take over the ship, but Lucas wouldn't mind getting him in trouble anyway. He hated that dude. Any kid acting like an adult needed an attitude adjustment. Or marooning on a deserted island.

"Go on now, lad. Go with the crew. They need their grog after a fight, or they be leery of joining in the next one. Billy and me'll set the course toward the household ye indercated. What fer patching the hull an' all." Flatus shooed Lucas down the steps.

"Wait, Captain—" Lucas said. Someone bumped into him, and he stumbled down a few more steps toward the galley. Flatus took off to the helm. The chance was lost.

Lucas went down to where the boisterous celebration was happening: the galley. There was a big stove with a copper kettle atop it that looked suspiciously like a luxury hotel sink. Along one wall were dozens of barrels. Low tables spread out across the big space, consisting mostly of random objects with planks on top. Chunks of barrels, crates, stools, flotsam and other sea garbage created seats for the pirates. More makeshift lanterns hung on metal pegs sticking out of the walls, swaying back and forth and casting eerie glows over the place. If it wasn't so noisy with happy chatter, it might have been creepy.

The cook was missing a foot, and his wooden leg's thump echoed off the walls even better than the laughter of pirates anticipating drink. Lucas eyeballed him. He looked familiar from their introduction earlier. He was a huge round man with grease smeared down his clothes and through his hair. He looked like a perfect match for the lunch lady who'd poisoned him with the bean burritos earlier. His stomach gurgled again. It would take some work to hold it in, but he'd much rather not poo in a bucket. Lucas sat down on a little wooden box in the corner.

"What's his deal?" Lucas said to the nearest pirate. It was Crudd, the one with the pet rat and epic dreadlocks.

"Huh? Oh y'mean ol' Thumper? He went an' got hisself shanked in the kneecap, that he did. Unpleasant way o' losing the leg, hard choices t'be made, but he found himself a place on the crew nonetheless," said Crudd.

"Oh. That sucks. So... how long have you been on the crew here?" Lucas asked.

"Off an' on since I was about your age, lad. Pirating is a contract job. Ye sign up jus' fer as long as ye want. If ye do well, might be Cap'n comes a callin' again. If not, might be ye get yer butt keelhauled before being unflushed back up top. I think I had me about twenty adventures as a lad, before signing on all permanent like. When things up top got less than merry," Crudd said.

Crudd's eyes glossed over. Lucas felt awkward, like he was intruding on some private thoughts. Crudd's hair was still orange even in the dark. He tucked it behind his shoulder, to the rat's squeaking protest.

"How old are ye, matey?" Crudd asked.

"Ten," Lucas said.

"Ah, ten. Thought so. Been jus' about ten years since I done joined up the crew here full time, aye," Crudd said.

"That's a long time to be in the sewers. Aren't you sick of it?" Lucas asked.

"Har! It ain't been ten years in the sewers. We be true pirates, not poop-encrusted pirates like some would say. The sewers be brilliant passages fer recruiting purposes. Cannot sail on the paved streets, after all. Used t'be there were a clear passage betwixt the sewer an' open sea. Used t'be. Meddlin' plumbers went an' sealed it up. Protecting the environment or some such malarkey. The *Scumbucket*'ll be back there soon, mark me words. On open seas again, fresh sea air an' all." Crudd seemed pretty hopeful.

Mugs were passed around. Crudd banged his on the plank table, and the rest of the group joined in. *Thump, thump, thump.* Lucas's head hurt, but he tried to make a little noise too. His mug looked like it was a toothbrush holder in a past life. A big keg of blue liquid was passed around next. Crudd poured himself a hearty portion and offered it to Lucas. Lucas knew what it was now; it burned his eyes. Mouthwash. He shook his head.

Crudd looked disappointed for a second but poured a little swig into Lucas's mug anyway. Lucas scrunched his nose as the jug got passed back the other way. Drinking mouthwash? Ugh. No way. Lucas felt nauseated all over again. Good thing he'd already vomited, or it might have come up all over the makeshift table. Maybe if he did drink the grog, at least his puke would be a pretty blue color and minty fresh.

"Food," someone roared amidst the thumping mugs.

"Hold yer horses, ye scurvy scum," Thumper hollered.

"If we've got scurvy, it's your fault," Viscous Val's nasally voice called out.

"Yar!" Thumper thumped his one-legged self over to a barrel and pried the lid off with a crowbar that looked like a shoehorn. Lucas thought he saw some cockroaches scurry out but looked away, rather than know for sure. He could resist the yucky pirate food today, but if he got stuck down here longer... he would be happier not knowing what had pooped on it. The cook chucked hockey-puck-sized things at the room.

"What are those?" He didn't really want to know. Lucas ducked as one whizzed past his ear.

"Urinal cakes." Crudd bit into one with a crunch.

"Urinal cakes?" Lucas choked.

Lucas turned green, spun around, and stuck his head between his knees. Mouthwash was one thing, but urinal cakes? The sickeningly sweet-smelling pink tablets of sanitation that everybody peed on? The lurching of the ship floating in the toilet water didn't help his plight. Lucas hiccupped. Crudd whacked him on the back a few times.

"Puke be a fitting name fer ye," Crudd laughed and laughed. Several of the pirates at their table joined in. Lucas wasn't thrilled to be the butt of their jokes, but he wasn't feeling well enough to argue.

Lucas finally sat up, the current wave of nausea passed. He still felt dizzy and flopped his face down on the table. He looked at the wall to avoid harassment from the pirates. There were some portholes along the wall, and Lucas studied them to pass the time. It was so dark and dreary outside that he couldn't see much. The thick water splashed at the portholes time and time again. Maybe this wasn't helping his stomach. It was like being flushed all over again.

Something moved and caught his eye outside. Lucas sat bolt upright, seasickness forgotten. It wasn't clear, a smoky outline at best. But he thought he saw —

"Did you see that?" Lucas asked Crudd.

"They be sea biscuits. Not urinal cakes. I got ye good, eh Puke?" Crudd ignored the question.

"Oh," he said. Lucas was almost embarrassed he had gotten sick over a lie but was distracted by whatever it was moving around outside the ship.

"Take a bite. An' rest assured, the best be yet to come. Rat jerky," Crudd said. His pet rat squealed in outrage.

Crudd pushed a biscuit toward him. Lucas shook his head. He couldn't get rid of the image of leaning into a urinal, picking up the pink tablet and crunching into it. Finding some hairs stuck on it. And rat jerky didn't sound any tastier than urinal cakes.

"Sorry, no. Excuse me —" Lucas tried to get up.

Crudd grabbed his arm and tugged him back down onto his box. Lucas sighed. Lucas wanted to shove this instance into the face of Mrs. Anthony. See? Saying *excuse me* wasn't a cure-all. It didn't open all doors. Some people didn't care about manners.

"Nay, stay till ye have a drink. It be good luck."

"I don't feel good, I need some air..."

"If ye don't celebrate the victory, ye might be labeled a mutineer. One o' the plumber scum, even. Jus' stay. Don't let it chap yer hiney." Crudd narrowed his eyes.

Lucas went white. Did he suspect Dad was a plumber? How could he have even—? Lucas swallowed and sat down.

"Huzzah!" Crudd shouted and raised his mug of mouthwash grog.

The rest of the room joined in, hoisting their mismatched mugs high and hollering huzzah a dozen times. Lucas tried to seem excited, lifting his arm a bit. His arm could barely support the weight of the little mug; he felt weak all over. Sea sickness? Maybe. Fear of being on the bad side of these pirates? Definitely.

The look Flatus had given him when he'd asked to go home wasn't very reassuring. He almost felt better hearing about Crudd's long history with the *Scumbucket*, having many contracts and going home between. Lucas might manage that. But this whole business about plumbers being the arch enemies of the sewer-sailors and Dad being a plumber... That was bad news. Not to mention Dad harping on and on, warning Lucas about them since before he could remember. It was a dangerous game he was playing, supping with the enemy.

Everyone around him chugged their grog and gargled noisily. The group-gargle was just about the weirdest thing Lucas had seen that day, and that said a lot. He put a little bit in his mouth and swished it around. Wintergreen, yum! It almost tricked his nose into ignoring the fecal smells all around him. Maybe that was why the pirates didn't mind living in the sewer.

Suddenly, all the pirates in the galley spun around and spat their blue grog out onto the floor. *Psshhhh.* Lucas's feet got splashed from all directions. He lifted them up. He didn't want the mixture of mouthwash and saliva on his bare feet. Yuck. He felt trapped and knew he'd have to walk out of there eventually.

Crudd reached over and slugged Lucas in the shoulder, making him choke on his grog instead of spew it out like the rest of the crew. Lucas coughed violently. It got all up in his sinuses and burned worse than spraying cola out his nose.

Lucas stood up from the table without asking for permission. It seemed the way of the pirate crew. He wanted to steal a peek over the ship's rail. Try to catch sight of the gator or whatever it was he saw earlier. And surprisingly, he felt a lot less sick post-mouthwash. Crudd let him go this time. He tiptoed around the table and back toward the stairs, disgusted with the sticky blue spit he walked through. His feet suctioned to the floorboards with every step. *Spish, Spish, Spish.*

Lucas took one last peek toward the porthole before he went to the upper deck. Against all odds, he saw it again. It was much clearer this time, and couldn't be mistaken for a gator. It was a face.

Chapter Five

"Hey! I saw you," Lucas yelled as he reached the railing. He ran up the stairs, despite his sticky, minty, mouthwash-coated feet. He wanted to catch the owner of the face on the opposite side of the porthole.

Lucas hung over the side, looking for the body to match the face he saw through the round window below deck. Flatus and Billy Rubin were on the poop deck, steering the *Scumbucket*. It seemed leagues away; they may mistake his yelling as spewing. The ship lurched to the side as they maneuvered. Lucas surprisingly wasn't nauseated. If mouthwash had stomach-settling effects, he might start using it at home. If he ever got back.

"Hello, sailor."

He heard a voice behind him and spun around like a ballerina. Skills. He had them. Lucas blinked a few times in the dim light before he made out a shadowy whisper of a figure on deck. It was obviously female, small, maybe a kid around Lucas's age. But she didn't move like a kid; she was graceful. Dark hair and shadowy skin, wrapped in a cloak long enough to tickle the deck's planks... He couldn't see her feet. Was she floating?

"Who are you? Why are you hanging around the ship?" Lucas asked.

"I like to visit new sailors. I want to meet you, to know you, as you are now. Before you become like the rest." She pointed below deck with a whispery shadow of a hand.

"Oh. That's kinda weird, but okay. I'm Puke."

"I know who you are. Your name isn't Puke. It's Lucas."

It was too dark to see her face, but Lucas heard her voice loud and clear. It sounded musical to his ears, despite the sloshing gunk lapping at the ship's hull. He wanted to know her, too. That sounded just swell. He was too curious to be creeped out and took a step closer.

"How do you know me? Who are you?" Lucas's heart stepped it up a notch.

"I'm a siren, we know things. Come with me." She held out her hand.

"What's your name?" Lucas asked.

His hand reached out to hers without thinking. He didn't know half of what she was talking about. Siren? Like blue and red police popcorn-lights? She ignored his question and didn't say her name.

"Come. Come now before the crew poisons you against me. Come, you'll like it down below, where I live. It's much more beautiful than here. All the foul things in the sewer float. Underneath, it's so serene. We'll be friends. The very best of friends." She reached toward his hand.

"Oh, okay. What's your town called?" Lucas couldn't take his eyes off her.

"It's called Ascaris."

"Ascaris..." Lucas parroted. Such an amazing name for a town. Lucas really wanted to know her actual name, not just her town's name, since she was so completely awesome.

"Please tell me your name? I really want to know." Lucas heard himself break into a whine.

"My name is Giardia." Her face was mostly shadow, but Lucas imagined she smiled as she said it.

He savored each syllable, *gee-arr-dee-ahhhhh*. "Giardia!"

He exhaled heavily. *Mmm...* such a dreamy name. Maybe Italian or something exotic. It all sounded pretty sweet to Lucas. He wasn't really into girls, but a magical sea creature trumped that logic.

Sudden pounding of feet over the deck snapped Lucas out of his trance. The pirate captain burst onto the scene and flailed his plunger toward the siren.

"Avast, ye vile bawdy wench. Off me ship, ye venomed dread-bolted demon of the night," Flatus yelled.

Billy Rubin came too and backed him up with two toothbrushes sharpened into daggers. The siren made a little sound, as though sighing sadly. Then, without warning, she vaporized into the dim sewer. Vanished—Like a silk scarf blowing away in the breeze.

"Hey! What are you doing?" Lucas whined. He reached over the railing toward where she went, grabbing at the air. Grasping at nothing.

Lucas wasn't sure why, but he really wanted to go with her. He ran his fingers through his hair viciously, without even noticing the scum built up on his scalp. He'd finally met someone magical and clean in this disgusting tube of a sewer, and Flatus had to go and run her off.

"Are you three sheets to the wind, Puke?" Billy Rubin asked.

"Huh? What about sheets? I just want to go see Ascaris..." Lucas couldn't translate that pirate-speak and was generally confused down here anyway. Why didn't the pirates like the siren? She was amazing. Pure magical perfection.

"Are you crazy?" Billy was obviously annoyed having to explain himself.

"Calm yeself, lad. Sirens are all infectious black magic and vexing voodoo, calling nice lads like yeself down to the deep. Ye far too young t'meet Davy Jones, Puke. Don't go down to the deep, Dingleberry. Stay topside with us." Flatus knelt to look Lucas in the eye.

"My name's not Dingleberry. Or Puke. Giardia knew that. She knew me." Lucas crossed his arms then uncrossed them again. He stomped around the deck. She invited him to see her town, but she wasn't going to drown him, surely. That was insanity.

"An' how do ye think she knew ye? Tricks. Mischief. An' not the good kind o' mischief neither," Flatus said.

"Whatever." Lucas spat the word at Flatus.

"Listen up, Puke. You will address the captain—your captain—with the utmost respect at all times. Understood?" Billy jabbed his spiked toothbrush toward Lucas's stomach.

Lucas swatted him away. He didn't care what these smelly swashbucklers thought about his manners. He wanted to go with the siren. She might have been the one girl in the universe who was interesting to Lucas, but now he'd never know. She was magical and wanted his company, not like Tabitha from class, who was neither magical nor interested in Lucas. Now Giardia was gone... Long gone. By the time she came back, Lucas would be beyond help. Stinky and disgusting like the rest of them. And she wouldn't want him then.

"Avast! Look at that hole in the hull. The poison-ous wench took a little souvenir to remember you by, Puke. The cost of that repair will be deducted from any booty or plunder you acquire, I assure you," Billy Rubin lectured Lucas.

Lucas shrugged. He didn't care what the siren did to the boat. The *Scumbucket* was full of scum and unwashed pirates. Giardia was full of better stuff. He didn't know what, but he felt pretty sure of it.

"Ease off there, mate. He be dizzy-eyed an' poi-soned with her sweet words. Give him a minute t'cool down, and he'll be right as rain." Flatus gestured to calm Billy.

"Aye-aye, Captain." Billy didn't sound convinc-ing.

"Come now, Puke, we be approaching that lass's house. Help us navigate. Yer rather good with maps," Flatus said.

Lucas didn't want to, but Flatus steered him an-yway. The more time passed the less Lucas felt like jumping over the side of the ship to follow the siren. His head felt clearer. By the time they got to the poop deck, Lucas felt like himself again. He snickered.

"Here now, Puke, know ye the address?" Flatus pulled out the sewer diagram again.

"No, but it's the third house on the left side of the street. On Marley Boulevard." Lucas took a look at the weak excuse for a treasure map again. He pointed out Tabitha's house easily.

"Aye. That'll do, Puke. Billy, ye has the helm. I'll be escorting young Puke here t'find the hull-patcher denture glue," Flatus said.

"Aye-aye, Captain. I will have the *Scumbucket* in position when you flush." Billy saluted.

"Um, can I just wait here?" Lucas asked.

"Listen up, you little Puke. You shall address the captain properly, or I will personally see to it you are marooned in a deep dark sewer pipe," Billy said.

Captain Flatus took off his pirate hat and handed it to Billy. The first mate looked way too happy about it and clutched it to his chest.

"Ease off there, Billy. Priorities an' all. Puke, nay, ye may not stay behind. How will I know where t'find the booty?"

Captain Flatus pulled out a fat pistol that looked like a mix between a cannon and a grappling hook. It had a spool of chain attached to it. Lucas gulped. The siren's hypnotic hold on him had faded, but jumping overboard with her still seemed preferable to whatever was about to happen.

"I'm not so sure about that thing, Captain... sir..." Lucas tried to be polite, but he was scared silly by that gun.

"Come now, stop with yer pribble. An away mission be the best remedy for that there auditory poison o'sewer sirens. Hang on t'me belt, Puke. Watch out fer the blunderbuss," Flatus said.

"The *Scumbucket* will be shipshape upon your return, Captain," Billy said.

"Aye. Hang on there, Puke. I be serious," Flatus said.

Flatus aimed the pistol-looking thing up at a drain hole in the ceiling of the cavernous sewer pipe. He maneuvered to one side to get the sails out of their line of sight before firing off a shot.

"If you return," Billy Rubin muttered under his breath. Lucas just barely caught his words. Had Flatus heard? This was one step away from the stupidity of villains monologuing before the hero was actually dead.

"Captain Flatus—Did you—"

That was Lucas's last conscious thought before he got hit with the g-force. His body went limp like a doll, yanked up into the air by a grappling hook, operated by a stinky old seadog.

Lucas came back to his senses on the floor of a fluffy pink bathroom. His face was planted in a frilly pink rug that smelled blissfully better than the *Scumbucket*. He groaned and looked up. Flatus was rummaging around through glossy white cabinets, looking much the same as when Lucas had first laid eyes on him.

Flatus's problem was throwing himself headfirst into whatever he was trying to pillage. Sometimes it was smarter to take a step back, think, and plan. Lucas saw the medicine cabinet on the wall, plain as day, but Flatus seemed to miss it entirely by climbing under the sink.

"It be not here! Where be the bilge-sucking, scurvy-ridden denture paste, Puke?"

Flatus spoke way too loud, and his face was red as a beet. He slammed the cabinet door a bit too fast, and it pinched his tangled blond hair. He yowled like an alley cat, and Lucas kicked him in the shin before he could think better of it. He needed to be quiet. Quiet was apparently scarce among pirate-kind.

"Hush! They'll hear you," Lucas said. Flatus rubbed his shin and glared at Lucas.

"Be it too much to ask fer a little bit o' respect, Puke? Billy seems t'think ye'll never make a proper pirate, and that—"

"If Billy Rubin is a proper pirate, I definitely don't want to be one. He's only sucking up to you because he wants to take the *Scumbucket* for himself. He's probably sabotaging us right now so he can just become captain and never see us again. That'd make him happy. Are you so oblivious that you can't even—"

"What's that sound?" A feminine voice floated through the closed door of the bathroom.

"Oh—Just trust me and be quiet," Lucas's heart beat faster than a drummer could pull off.

"Arrrr..." Flatus growled.

"Sir. Captain, sir," Lucas gave it an honest try, being polite.

The captain scowled but stayed quiet. If Flatus took the accusation of his first mate seriously, Lucas vowed to try harder at the pirate-version of respect. With the aye-ayes and the shipshapes. Sometime when Tabitha wouldn't hear them plundering her bathroom, preferably.

"I don't hear anything, Honey Bear," said a granny-type voice.

After fearing for his life a few seconds, Lucas relaxed. He scrambled up and looked around, taking care to be quiet. This did appear to be where Granny did her duty; there was a metal bar on the wall alongside the tub and toilet, like a handicap bathroom stall. There was also a little chair in the shower, peeking out from behind a frilly lace shower curtain. Grandma stuff.

"Try there, in the medicine cabinet," Lucas whispered and pointed to the mirrored box on the wall.

Flatus nodded and reached up. He pulled it open as gently as his meaty hands could manage. There were all number of things inside there: amber vials of pills from the pharmacy, glass bottles of perfumes, and, yes, a partially-used economy-sized tube of denture glue. Flatus scooped out the entire shelf into a sack. The noise was horribly loud.

"Granny! Turn up your hearing aid. There's a noise," Tabitha said from the hall.

"What?" Granny answered back.

"A noise, in the bathroom. I'll go look."

Tabitha's footsteps sounded closer to the bathroom door. Lucas panicked, ready to flip out. The last thing he needed was Tabitha thinking him a creepy stalker, who hung out in Granny's bathroom stealing her weird grandma stuff. He wasn't sure he could think of a good explanation for that. And then there was Flatus. He was entirely beyond explanation.

"Go, go, go," Lucas barked in a hurried whisper.

Captain or not, he had to stop being such an imbecile if he wanted respect. The instant he became a quick and savvy pirate, then he could have all the aye-ayes on the planet. Lucas reached up and locked the door in a burst of intelligence. It wasn't a second too soon. Tabitha's hand grabbed it on the other side and wiggled the brass knob.

"What... that's weird," Tabitha said to herself.

"What's that, Honey Bear?" Granny said.

"Oh, the door must have gotten locked somehow. I'll just grab the key real quick."

Tabitha started jumping up and down outside the door. Thump, thump, thump. Lucas thought she was mad as a hatter until he realized what she was doing. She was getting the key that people always kept on the top of the doorframe. He hoped she was way too short to grab it. His stomach flipped over with fear that she wasn't.

"C'mon," Lucas jumped into the toilet and motioned to Flatus. Water sloshed out and soaked the fluffy pink rug.

"Oh, that be a real gem, that be..." Flatus locked his eyes on the toilet's padded pink cushioned seat. There was even pink carpet attached to the tank.

"Let it go, Flatus. We got what we came for."

"Get out o' there, ye mewling lad. I'll be plundering that if ye don't mind." Flatus said.

"We have to go now. Even if Tabitha catching us doesn't bother you, maybe Billy Rubin's mutiny of the *Scumbucket* would perk you up? I'll bet he's doing it right now. Telling the crew we died, and they're headed out for open sea like they all want. Billy's probably blaming you for keeping them stuck in the sewers for all this time."

Flatus plucked Lucas out of the toilet and set him dripping on the fluffy pink rug. If Lucas wasn't halfway to crazy, he might have applauded the feat of strength. As it stood, he wished Flatus would've just gotten them out of there. Pirates and logic didn't mix.

"Enough of yer hornswaggling. Maybe Billy were right about ye. Not fit as a pirate." Flatus wouldn't look Lucas in the eye.

"Seriously? You're going to believe that kid instead of—"

The door swung open. Tabitha stared straight at Lucas.

"Uh, hey," Lucas said to Tabitha.

Lucas figured she would spaz out now. They stared at each other silently for an eon, before he realized she wasn't even staring at him anymore. She stared over his shoulder, directly at the pirate captain.

Lucas moved his body in an attempt to block Flatus ripping the fancy toilet seat off its bolts. He held out his arms awkwardly, pretending to yawn or lean on the countertop.

Tabitha didn't blink.

"Oh, I wasn't expecting... you." Tabitha's voice was quiet and nonplussed.

Well, that was a much milder response than Lucas braced himself for.

"Surprise?" Lucas tried to smile.

"Avast!" Flatus said.

The captain dropped his work on the toilet seat and unsheathed his plunger cutlass. He pointed it right at Tabitha's guts and gave her a full view of his dirty face and crazy eyes.

"Hello." Tabitha didn't seem nearly disturbed enough.

"Avast?" Flatus repeated, less sure of himself this time. He retracted his plunger.

"A vast what? Are you Lucas's dad?" Tabitha asked.

Lucas was dumbstruck. Not only did this chick think he was disgusting, she thought Flatus, the most disgusting creature on the face of the planet, was his dad. Tabitha thought that Lucas had been spawned by a filthy, sewer-sailing, scum-sucking pirate captain. Lucas's head hurt.

"You must be Lucas's dad. I'm Tabitha. We're in the same class. I like your tattoo," Tabitha said.

"He's not—" Lucas wanted to set the record straight but stopped himself. His eye started twitching. This wasn't the worst misunderstanding possible. It'd be worse if Tabitha suspected the truth: pirates were plundering her bathroom.

"Not what?" Tabitha asked.

"Uh—" Lucas's voice wasn't there for him, for perhaps the first time in history. He usually talked too much, not too little.

"You said your dad was a plumber, but it didn't click that maybe he'd be working at our house sometime. Granny has had the Viking Plumbers magnet on our fridge ever since they met at some PTA thing." Tabitha shrugged.

"Yeah… small world, right?" Lucas forced a smile, despite being on the verge of a panic attack. He didn't want Flatus to know Dad was a plumber. He didn't want to be stuck in a life-or-death situation with someone whose sworn enemy was a close relation of his. He couldn't argue the point. He was stuck between a radioactive rock and a hard place with laser cannons.

"A plumber?" Flatus looked up from his booty. His cheeks flushed bright red.

"We'll be finishing up soon. Don't let us interrupt your TV show. Don't even bother Granny with this. We'll clean everything up." Lucas tried to dismiss Tabitha. He held his breath.

"Granny hasn't made a peep since I've been in here. That's a sure sign she's asleep in her chair. When did she let you in, anyway? I didn't notice."

"A while ago. Not too long ago. Earlier…?" Lucas wasn't sure what the right answer was. Whatever it was, it wasn't the truth. The truth was most definitely the wrong answer.

"You get pretty dirty, being a plumber. I guess that wouldn't bother you, though." Tabitha scanned Flatus and Lucas in turn.

Lucas agreed; he was filthy. "Oh yeah, so filthy. Covered in scum. Saturated with essence of toilet water! You'd hate being a plumber. You should probably just look away before you're traumatized by this." Lucas grabbed the thread he'd been given and ran.

"Are you being sexist?" Tabitha lowered her voice and growled.

"What? No. Who in their right mind likes getting dirty? I hate it, but, uh, Dad really needed me to—" Lucas said.

"Liar. You think just because I'm a girl I don't want to get dirty. Well, you're wrong." Tabitha rolled up the sleeves of her fuzzy pink fleece pajamas like she meant business.

"Well, you're always complaining about my bodily functions—" Lucas lowered his voice. Not that he needed to, Flatus was making a huge racket dismantling the toilet. Somehow the shower curtain had come down and gone into his sack, too.

"I don't care if you've got bad gas in class. I saw what the cafeteria was serving. I care that you talk about it all the time and are so proud of it. Ever heard of manners?"

"Oh." Lucas frowned and failed to formulate a response.

"Step lively now, matey," Flatus said.

Lucas looked over at him, thankful for distraction from the awkwardness with Tabitha. The big pirate stepped in the toilet and beckoned Lucas. He looked like a pirate Santa Claus with his sack of plunder on his back. The pink toilet seat looped around his shoulder like a trendy new purse.

Lucas was afraid to look back at Tabitha, considering she was also seeing the complete and utter ridiculousness of Flatus Codswallup. And she thought this was Dad. Lucas twitched. He was unsure whether to run to Flatus and get flushed down into poopville again, or run past Tabitha and out the front door toward home.

"Tabitha," Lucas spun back toward her. He thought of ten-thousand things to say to explain the awkward situation but shot them all down before they came out of his mouth. He gurgled like a goldfish on carpet.

"Only people I hate call me Tabitha," she snapped.

"Oh. Well what do you wanna be called?" Lucas threw up his arms. The girl acted like she didn't see the pirate in her dismantled pink toilet. Pure insanity.

"Tab. My friends call me Tab," she said.

"So can I call you Tab?"

"No, we're not friends." Tabitha raised an eyebrow and pointed toward Flatus, impatiently waiting in the toilet bowl. "Have you been swimming in the sewer? Or just wading in my toilet?"

"You have no clue." Lucas laughed.

Flatus reached over and grabbed Lucas's shirt. Lucas watched Tabitha's face turn from bemused to alarmed as Lucas got hoisted from the pink-carpeted rug to the pink toilet bowl. What would she think when they went down the drain?

Then, Flatus flushed. At least this toilet was clean.

Chapter Six

"What are you doing, Mr. Goodspeed?" Tabitha sounded awkward, like she felt weird for asking.

Lucas opened his eyes that were clamped tight to prevent pinkeye during the flush. They were still in froufrou-pink, lacy bathroom-land. Apparently the flush had failed. Flatus still held onto Lucas's shirt with a death grip, and both of their feet were ankle-deep in toilet water.

Lucas laughed at Tabitha. Not for asking, but for acting like she'd been in the wrong for bringing it up. There were two smelly, crusty pirates standing in her toilet, and she felt silly for asking what's going on. If this was where manners got her, why would Lucas want any for himself?

"Flusher be busted," Flatus said.

"Probably because Billy Rubin took over the *Scumbucket* and sailed her far, far away from here." Lucas started the sentence quiet, to shield from Tabitha's ears, but realized it was a tiny bathroom, and there was no chance of that. He hoped she assumed Lucas was crazy and hadn't actually listened.

"I know the flusher is busted. That's why we called you to come fix it," Tabitha laughed.

"Or, Puke, the flusher be busted. The more likelier o' the two," Flatus said.

"Whatever— Wait a sec. You called us?" Lucas started to dismiss Flatus's hypothesis when Tabitha's words slapped him silly. What was she talking about? She dialed up the Drain-Navy on the USS *Scumbucket*?

"Obviously," Tabitha said, all snippily with an upturned nose.

"And, um, who is us?" Lucas stumbled out of the toilet onto the pink rug and dripped.

"Viking Plumbers. Obviously. That's why I mentioned the magnet on our fridge."

It finally clicked in Lucas's mind. That was why she hadn't freaked out finding two dudes in her bathroom. That was why she seemed to be expecting someone working on her toilet. She had called the plumbers. She had called the Viking Plumbers. With their dumb Viking hats and stupid Viking shirts and—Dad.

"C'mon, um, duh, we gotta get going. Let's go back to the uh, van and get the flusher-fixer thing." Lucas stuttered with panic. He was not interested in running into Dad here. That would take awkward and raise it to the level of mind-blowingly insanely awkward. He tried to call Flatus *Dad* but failed miserably. His mouth wouldn't say it, even in farce.

"You don't have the right tools in that giant sack?" Tabitha pointed to Flatus's plunder bag.

"It be requirin' a special sort o' tool, ye pint-sized wench," Flatus spoke up.

Lucas laughed. Flatus's grammar-free assault on Tabitha was priceless.

"Just so you know, I write Granny's checks for her. And you won't be getting any payment until this toilet works flawlessly." Tabitha raised her voice.

"Obviously." Lucas parroted Tabitha's annoying word-of-choice right back at her.

Flatus finally gave up on the flusher when it snapped off in his thick fingers. He shrugged, pocketed the brass lever, and stepped out of the toilet bowl.

"Aye, Puke. Have t'find another portal to the *Scumbucket*," Flatus said.

"Yes! We'll be right back, Tabitha. Don't even bother waking up Granny. We'll leave quietly and come back inside very, very quietly," Lucas said. Even if Tabitha was dumb enough to think pirates were plumbers, he doubted the misunderstanding would carry over to Granny if she woke up.

"Only I call my grandmother *Granny*, Lucas."

Lucas started to ask what to call her, but decided he didn't care. Granny was much easier to remember than anything Tabitha would say. She'd probably told Lucas Granny's name last time he was here, but he'd forgotten ninety-nine percent of what he'd learned that day.

Tabitha led Flatus and Lucas to the front door like a good host. They went past the TV room where Granny snored up a storm in front of an infomercial. Lucas tiptoed instinctively to avoid waking Granny. Flatus seemed to get noisier than ever, his toilet-water-soaked boots squeaking and sack of plunder jangling. Lucas clenched his teeth.

None of that made Granny miss a snore. Lucas was just about to be relieved when the doorbell sounded. *Darrrriiinnggg-dong*. His heart skipped a beat-and-a-half. Granny's snore was severed, and she sat up in her recliner.

"The plumber is here, Honey Bear," Granny called.

Flatus pulled out his plunger-sword.

Lucas gulped.

"What's going on?" Tabitha's eyes darted from Lucas to Flatus to Granny to the front door.

"Viking Plumbers emergency service," a muffled voice called through the door.

"Um—" Lucas tried to think fast. What explanation could he conjure up? Extra help? Backup? Ha, like the plumbers were cops requesting backup. As if.

"Avast!" Flatus jabbed his spiked plunger toward the closed front door.

"Couldn't fix the toilet on our own, had to call in backup," Lucas blurted out.

"Where be the nearest sewer portal, lass?" Flatus knelt down and questioned Tabitha eye-to-eye.

"Sewer portal? You mean manhole? I didn't know the technical term for them was portal. Makes me think of those video games with the giant pipes." Tabitha chuckled.

Lucas held his breath. This could not actually be working out.

"What be a video game? Where be this manhole ye speak of?" Flatus asked again. His plunger still pointed toward the door, and urgency tinted his voice.

"Right outside, really. In the middle of the street straight down the driveway. I didn't realize our clog was that horrible. Before you fix it, can you give me a written estimate? I'll have to discuss it with Granny before investing too much toward the repairs."

The doorbell rang a few times more. Tabitha narrowed her eyes at Lucas. Lucas stared back at her. His heart threatened to pop out of his chest, but he attempted to keep his cool. She unlatched and opened the door and let it swing all the way open.

"Hello, miss. I'm Carl Goodspeed from Viking—Lucas?" Dad said.

Lucas's dad stood framed in the door and backlit from the yellow streetlight. His horned Viking helmet was lame, even silhouetted with dusk. His son could recognize his lumpy profile anywhere, even without his telltale voice. Lucas made an awkward wave at his dumbfounded dad.

"You!" Carl pointed over Lucas's shoulder at Flatus Codswallup. They knew each other?

Tabitha's gears turned, her beady little eyes zipping back and forth from the plumber to the pirate to Lucas. She'd figure this out soon. Too soon.

"Thanks for letting the plumbers in, Honey Bear," Granny said sleepily from the other room. All eyes looked her way. The group was jumpy. Lucas was surprised nobody had been run-through by the plunger yet. When Granny started snoring again, removing herself from the list of present threats, insanity unfurled.

"What are you doing with my son?" Dad took a step through the door. He ignored Tabitha and Lucas entirely, moving past them slowly toward Flatus. He unhooked a huge metal wrench from his tool belt and slapped it into his other hand.

"Yer son? So it be true. Puke, fess up! Yer a two-faced double-crosser." Flatus held his plunger toward Dad but waggled his opposite finger at Lucas.

"What? You kidnapped me! I never asked to join your stinky crew of buttcaneers," Lucas said.

"Buccaneers?" Tabitha said. A lot of crazy talk was slung around, but the word buttcaneers took the cake. Of course the butt pun went over her head. She inched backward toward the TV room and her snoring granny.

Unfortunately for Tabitha, her movement took her too close to Flatus's grubby pirate arm. Flatus scooped up her orange-headed self in a quick maneuver.

"Hey," Tabitha yelped. She kicked and squirmed, but Flatus's grip held tight.

"Whoa now, she's just a kid. Put her down, pirate," Dad said.

Dad made a show of setting down his plumber wrench. A gesture of good will.

Lucas froze. He hadn't known Flatus to be violent, but he had known him to be a kidnapper. Lucas didn't want Tabitha stuck in the same position as he was.

"Yeah, put her down Flatus," Lucas said.

"Who is this guy? I thought he was your dad, Lucas. Liar!" Tabitha was amazingly mean despite everything. She was a firecracker.

Dad put his hands up in a non-threatening pose. He babbled something soothing to Flatus. He wouldn't fight him; he'd let him go; just let the girl go. Lucas wasn't paying attention to Dad at the moment. He had bigger fish to fry, and he had remembered just the tool to do it with.

Lucas reached down to the useful cargo shorts loops Flatus had repurposed into holsters earlier. He tightened his grip on the spray bottle of bleach solution. He moved slowly, purposefully, waiting for his chance...

"Avast!" Lucas yelled. He whipped the bottle out and pulled the trigger. A stream of nuclear-green cleaning detergent flew right into Flatus Codswallup's face.

"Arrrr! Ye mutinous villainous Dingleberry," Flatus roared as he flailed around. His plunger-cutlass clattered on the tile entryway of Tabitha's house.

"Get back, Lucas," Dad moved closer to the writhing pirate, trying to grab the girl. Unfortunately for Tabitha, Flatus had her clamped tight like shackles.

"Let her go, Flatus," Lucas said. He tried to take aim for another shot to the pirate's eyeballs, but Flatus's fist was scrubbing them so violently he wasn't sure it'd have any effect.

"Help me," Tabitha ordered.

Lucas almost smiled. She wasn't squealing or crying but demanding she be saved. Lucas was inappropriately amused by the situation. But despite his smirk, he didn't want her to be thrown into the sewers like he'd been. They should both be free to take showers and breathe fresh air. He wasn't going to let her be taken. Nope.

"Flatus, you jerk. Haven't you ever considered finding willing recruits? What's with all this kidnapping crap?" Lucas said. He strafed around, trying to get a clear shot at the pirate's eyes again.

"It be the way of pirates. I take me prizes and me recruits with force, then once their conscience adjusts, they enjoy the life. Who wouldn't want t'be a pirate? Most do." Flatus got one red eye open and stared at Lucas.

"Ahhh!" Dad yelled out a Viking war cry and launched himself onto Flatus.

Carl Goodspeed was a pretty big man. He was above-average height, plenty of padding around the middle, but he was dwarfed compared to Flatus Codswallup. Lucas hadn't realized just how big Flatus was. Maybe six-and-a-half feet and not skinny. Lucas couldn't imagine eating enough urinal cakes and rat jerky to get fat. Pizza might be worth it, but not pirate chow. Dad clung like a champ for a moment before Flatus tossed him off and made a dash for the door.

Flatus grabbed the discarded wrench with his free hand and hefted it up like a tiny twig. He managed to keep a firm hold on Tabitha under the other arm and made short work of the front steps toward the portal.

"Forget ye, Dingleberry. There be plenty o' recruits in place of ye. Like yer friend here. Yer a fool fer giving up the pirate life," Flatus yelled as he ran away.

"Flatus, no," Lucas yelled. He started to follow them out the door when he felt a hand grab his ankle. He fell, hard.

"Lucas! Don't you dare chase him," Dad said.

Dad had successfully stopped Lucas's impulsive sprint out the door. Lucas felt bruises blossoming on both his kneecaps as testament to the fact.

"I can't let him take Tabitha. It's disgusting down there." Lucas got to his feet.

"I'm sorry about your friend, but there's nothing you can do. I'm not letting the sewer pirates get you." Dad pulled himself off the floor and adjusted his Viking hat.

"Uh, Dad? They already got me. That's why I'm soaked in sewer juice. Why do you hate them, anyway? I mean, I know why I hate them, but what about you? They don't seem totally evil. Kinda goofy, really," Lucas said.

"Lucas. What do you think I do as a plumber? What's my job, to you?" Dad asked.

76

"Seriously, Dad? We're going to chitchat right now? Tabitha is getting flushed." Lucas tried for the door again. Dad grabbed his wrist and held on tight.

"Do I look like I'm joking?" Dad's eyes were wild. Despite his crooked, fake-Viking trucker hat and his untucked dirty shirt, he looked as serious as a heart attack.

"I dunno. Unclog drains or something?" Lucas couldn't see Flatus and Tabitha anymore. They had disappeared into the dusky street, and the Viking Plumbers' van blocked the view.

"Yes, I fight clogs. And do you know what the biggest, baddest, most notorious clog is in this city? A pirate ship. A pirate ship, called the *Scumbucket*."

"Seriously? Your day job is dueling pirates in the sewers?" Lucas was skeptical.

"Yes. It is also my night job, since they started recruiting kids to join their crew. Kidnapping kids. Kidnapping you, Lucas. Do you think I can just let that happen? No. Not while I have breath left in my body." Dad monologued like a superhero. Lucas would have been embarrassed if anyone else had been listening to this.

"So? Go save Tabitha then. You think you're some sort of hero, do something about it," Lucas pointed out the door and whined at the top of his lungs.

"Do you need something, Mr. Plumber?" Granny hollered from the TV room. Lucas's heart stopped. He'd forgotten she was there.

"Have to go pick up some more parts, Mrs. Scott. Will return shortly." Dad didn't drop his death grip on Lucas's wrist as he led them outside.

"Very good now, dear. I'll just lock up behind you," Granny said. She got up and shuffled across the wood floor. *Prrott, prrott, prrott.*

Lucas and Dad stared wide-eyed at Tabitha's grandmother propelling her way across the house. Lucas snorted.

"Oh my! I've got the walkin' toots somethin' fierce," Granny said before shutting the door in their faces.

"Uh..." Lucas looked at Dad, forgetting the severity of their situation for the moment. They both snorted laughs for a few seconds before Dad straightened up.

"Let's go." Dad recovered his serious face. He hadn't let go of his death grip on Lucas. Dad hadn't forgotten anything, granny poots or no.

A loud clanking came from the street behind the big ugly plumber van. Someone had written *Wash Me* in the dirt on one side. Dad dragged Lucas by the wrist toward the van. Lucas wondered if anyone would call the cops and report a kidnapping; they must look fairly suspicious.

"Dad, c'mon. Let's go grab Tabitha before that idiot Flatus figures out how to open the manhole," Lucas said in a loud whisper.

Dad was smart enough not to engage in the argument. The silence drove Lucas mad. Especially when a struggling and grunting Tabitha was just yards away. Inches from being kidnapped and recruited as a pirate. A gong noise sounded. *Claaannnggg.* Lucas knew the pirate had wrenched open the heavy manhole cover and sent it flapping onto the ground. There were only seconds to act.

Dad's plan to kidnap his own son to protect him from pirates may have worked, if the van hadn't been locked. His keys were in the pocket closest to Lucas. When he maneuvered to fish them out, Dad lost his grip. It only took a split second. Lucas jerked his wrist away and dashed around the back of the van toward the manhole.

"Lucas, no. No." Carl stumbled after him, just in time to watch his kid tumble headfirst into the sewers.

Chapter Seven

About half a second into the free fall Lucas regretted his decision. The regret was quintupled when he landed face first in sewer juice.

After a few flails and scissor kicks, he rotated himself under the thick brown water and swam upward for his life. He didn't dare open his eyes. He'd had enough cases of pinkeye to know better.

Lucas may have thought the sewer water looked like gooey quicksand, but he was wrong. The goop keeping the *Scumbucket* afloat proved to be water. There was a benefit here being barefoot, since Lucas wasn't sure how well he'd have swum with sneakers on.

His head broke through the surface quicker than expected, but he didn't pull a mermaid-style gasp for breath. Lucas actually debated whether to sit there and suffocate rather than breathe in toilet water. His survival instinct eventually took over after he'd wiped the chunkier bits off of his face and blasted some gunk out of his nose. *Whooosh.* The breath felt sweet despite the rancid odor that came in with the air.

His eyes opened even slower than his mouth, only a tiny slit of one eye risking the bacteria infesting the sewer system. He peeked around cautiously in the murk and found himself face-to-face with a toothy sewer beast.

"Aaaahhh!" Lucas's eyes flew open like they were screaming too.

Squeeeeak. It was only a fat rat, leering at him from a ledge. Lucas scolded himself for being startled, and his eyes started to burn worse than his lungs.

The rat ran off in response to Lucas's caterwauling and didn't stop. Lucas's voice echoed after it, sounding farther and farther away in the sewer. It sounded like the indoor swimming pool where Lucas had taken swimming lessons as a kid, with the echoes and water droplet sounds amplified. He hadn't thought to be thankful for those lessons until now. Lucas made a mental note to thank Mom when he got back for saving him from drowning. If he got back.

"Lucas!" Dad's voice replicated itself in the sewer echo chamber, and Lucas heard his name about a hundred times.

"I'm alive," Lucas choked out. He struggled against the slippery goo, coating every solid surface in the sewer.

"Ahoy! It be a floater," Flatus's voice joined the echo-fest.

"You leave my son alone, pirate." Lucas knew Dad's veins were bulging out of his neck even though it was way too dark to see them.

"Finders, keepers, plumber scum. I be rescuing him. That be a debt he must repay on me crew," Flatus said. Apparently he hadn't written Lucas off as a traitor quite yet. The swan dive had maybe helped in that regard. Had it been worth it? Probably not, according to the full-body slime-coating.

"No!" Dad's voice wavered, like maybe he was going to give up. Lucas's stomach churned, half from that thought and half from the sludge in his mouth.

Lucas slung his arm over the concrete edge of the slow-moving waterway and hauled himself out of the filth. Just like swimming lessons. He sat his butt on the ledge and started dripping. Where was Flatus? Where was Tabitha? Had they already crawled out of the sewer water? Where was Dad? It sounded like he was up above somewhere, hidden in the shadows of the dark sewer pipe. Lucas sighed; Dad definitely hadn't jumped in after him.

Something whizzed through the air and smacked Lucas on the back of the head. It was the pink toilet seat, plundered from Tabitha's toilet, attached to a long grubby rope. He yelped.

"Don't hurt him. I'm coming for you, pirate, and I'm bringing back-up. You just wait, you just wait— You'll regret touching my son!" Dad hollered.

Dad's voice started to fade as he yelled. It sounded like he was leaving, moving away from the portal. Lucas wasn't sure what to think. He'd be back, of course. Wouldn't he? Lucas didn't need saving, anyway. Dad could take his time. He fought to clear the idea that Dad was too scared to jump in after his son. He didn't like that thought.

Lucas grabbed the toilet seat, bit his lip to stifle any more embarrassing yelps or cries, and threw it back the direction it had come from. Stupid Flatus Codswallup. It came right back like a boomerang and whacked Lucas between the shoulder blades.

"Stop it," Lucas was in a foul mood. Where was Tabitha, anyway? She better be alive if he was enduring all this just to save her.

"Grab on, matey. This is a rescue. Glad t'see ye came to yer senses. Welcome back to pirate life. Forget the plumber scum. Ye can apologize fer me eyeballs later," Flatus said.

Lucas dug his fists into his eye sockets. The itchy-burny feeling drove him batty. His foul mood took over, and he decided he'd deserved it after shooting cleaning spray into Flatus's eyes. He hadn't regretted the attack until the captain had welcomed him back. Apparently they weren't enemies, after all.

Lucas drug his feet up and out of the goo. He swiveled around, looking for the source of Flatus's voice.

"Where are you, Flatus?" Lucas shivered. It was cold being soaked through, underground, after night-fall. It couldn't get much worse.

"Grab onto the lifesaver, an' I'll reel ye in," Flatus said.

"Idiot! I'm already out of the water," Lucas said.

He grabbed the toilet seat and threw it back again with all his strength. He regretted his decision to leap into the sewer more and more. Now he was disgusting, wet, and had bruises on his head and back. Brilliant.

"You shouldn't talk to the captain that way, Lucas," Tabitha said.

Lucas leaped up and whirled toward the sound of Tabitha's voice. He was livid.

"No freaking way. You too? We're covered in poop in the sewer, and I'm *still* not allowed any backtalk? Don't you think that's the least bit messed up?" Lucas yelled.

"Well, you're sure covered in poop," Tabitha said.

Flatus and Tabitha finally got close enough for Lucas to see them. They were clean, all right. Well, Tabitha was clean. Flatus looked as dirty as ever but not like he'd been dunked like Lucas.

"What in the world? How did you—" Lucas said.

"There's a ladder built into the wall there," Tabitha pointed out.

"Ye must be crazy, Dingleberry, diving like that. Ye could've been killed," Flatus said.

Flatus leaned down and smacked Lucas on the back, hard. Lucas flailed, trying to whack away the pirate's hand. He was not amused.

"He was in a serious hurry to get down here after us. You weren't trying to rescue me, were you?" Tabitha asked.

Lucas searched her words for any hint of meanness. He thought he heard some sarcasm and scowled at her.

"No way. We're not even friends, like you said," Lucas snapped.

"Yeah. I didn't think so. Still glad you're not dead, even if we're not friends," Tabitha said.

"Thanks?" Lucas gave it a questioning lilt. He dug his fists back into his eyes. They itched worse than sneezing into a jar of chili powder.

"Don't cry now, Puke. Man up," Flatus hollered.

"I'm not crying. I've got pinkeye," Lucas whined. He thought maybe he was crying, but that was one of the smarter things his eyes had done lately. Flying open in fear of a sewer rat was one of the dumber things. Thanks, eyes.

"An eye infection? I'm not surprised. Don't touch your eyes. You'll make it worse and spread it. It's super contagious," Tabitha said.

"Shut up. And hey—How come you're not fighting to escape anymore?" Lucas asked. He looked between Flatus and Tabitha accusingly. Were they playing him somehow?

"Respect the wee lass. She be a fellow crewmate now, Puke." Flatus grabbed Lucas's shoulder hard.

"Captain Codswallup has been telling me about the lucrative benefits of becoming a sewer pirate. Part time, only. I told him I'd give it a shot, if it doesn't interfere with school. Granny could use a little padding to her Social Security checks." Tabitha's voice was quiet, maybe ashamed. Lucas ignored it.

"Money? You're going to pay Tabitha for this nightmare? You never paid me anything," Lucas snapped at Flatus.

"Respect the captain, Lucas," Tabitha said. Lucas felt his face flush.

"Yer booty be coming to ye, Puke. Now that this plunder be mine." Flatus shook the bag of loot he'd lifted from Tabitha's house.

"I'll believe it when I see it," Lucas said.

"Here we go, little matey. Hold still an' lemme wash that filth off of ye…" Flatus said.

"Huh?" Lucas looked up at the pirate questioningly. What was he going to —

"*Yeaahhhhhggg!*" Lucas hollered at the top of his lungs.

If he thought his eyes were burning bad before, he was sorely mistaken. Flatus doused him in grog to clean him off. Burny, minty mouthwash.

Lucas's pride had been wounded time and time again on this swashbuckling sewer adventure. But as it stood, it was the lowest low he could ever recall. He'd lost his shoes in the initial flushing and lost the rest of his clothes just now as Flatus ordered him to strip.

Lucas was beaten, wet and dirty and infected. He couldn't help but obey the captain's orders. The clothes were soaked through with every foul liquid known to man. In lieu of clothes, he donned the sack previously carrying Flatus's plunder. Lucas assumed it had been a high-quality pillowcase in a past life, and he felt surprisingly good and clean in it. The only annoyance was that it felt like wearing a dress. That sensation increased when Flatus offered the rag off his head to tie around his middle like a sash.

Tabitha was a surprisingly good sport when she saw all the stuff they'd plundered from her bathroom. Flatus didn't try to hide it and dumped everything onto the ground. He picked the best things to put in his pockets. Tabitha was determined to go through with this piracy thing. Lucas figured he'd never understand girls. Ever.

"Wh-wh-where's the *Scumbucket*?" Lucas asked. His teeth still chattered even though he was mostly dry. And his bare feet on cold concrete were kinda painful.

"Don't ye worry about that. Just get movin, lubber." Flatus shot him a look.

"Captain?" Lucas was too exhausted and violated by the sewer to rebel.

Flatus didn't notice his attempt at manners, and Lucas deflated.

The captain wasn't happy to see Billy Rubin had done just as Lucas had predicted. The *Scumbucket* was nowhere in sight. Flatus scowled under his breath and picked up his pace downstream.

Lucas tried to think warm thoughts and rubbed his hands together for friction. Flatus's long strides quickly left Lucas and Tabitha straggling behind. Lucas tried jogging to catch up but decided he'd be a gentleman for once and stick alongside Tabitha. They were in a creepy, stinky, dark, musty sewer, after all. No one in their right mind would want to be alone in these conditions. He kept his eyes on Flatus—getting lost would be a disaster. They walked and walked and walked. Lucas's bare feet felt raw and sore. He eyed Tabitha's pink house slippers enviously.

"How long have you been a pirate?" Tabitha broke the silence.

"I'm not a pirate," Lucas said.

"What? Flatus said you were on his crew," Tabitha's voice rose several octaves.

"No. Yes. No. Maybe."

"I thought that if you were on the crew at least, it wouldn't be so completely insane to come into the sewers and be a pirate. But if you're not even a pirate, who will I know? Who will I talk to? Who will look out for me?" Tabitha's voice morphed, slowly but surely, from frightened to mean.

"It'll be okay." Lucas didn't really believe it himself, but he had to try. If everything was really all right, he might have teased Tabitha into believing her fears. As it stood, he didn't want to believe her fears, either. Tabitha made a noise like she was gearing up to yell, and Lucas braced himself.

"Okay? It'll be okay? This is all your fault, Lucas." Tabitha's features mutated on her angry face.

"You're the toughest girl I know. You can take care of yourself." Lucas shrugged.

"Well, you're the most disgusting boy I know, so I'm sure you fit right in down here."

"Actually, not so much. The whole thing with Dad being a plumber is making it awkward. Sworn enemies and all. And Flatus seems to think I have a problem with authority."

"You do have a problem with authority."

"Shut up."

"And you're a hypocrite if you think I'm mean."

"Whatever." She was right, but he didn't feel like owning up to his own shortcomings. Being polite to the captain was bad enough. He was at odds with Flatus, Dad, and Mrs. Anthony. Maybe he was just a disagreeable dude. That's how it was starting to look, anyway.

"Where's Captain?" Tabitha ignored Lucas's dismissive remark. Lucas thought about the door on Flatus's cabin. *W.C.* Either Billy Rubin had been flat wrong about the meaning, or the entire crew of pirates were idiots. Maybe both explanations were true.

"What do you mean? He's right—"

But he wasn't right there. They were alone in the sewer.

"This is your fault, Lucas," Tabitha said.

"In what universe is this my fault? Flatus kidnapped you. Then suddenly you decide you want to be a pirate? That makes it anyone's fault but mine. I jumped into poo to get you out of this, you know," Lucas said.

"Aha! I knew you were trying to rescue me. I'm not sure whether to be disgusted or just confused." Tabitha's tone made it sound like she leaned toward disgusted. Lucas was hoping for amazed or impressed, or even grateful.

"Howzabout awestruck?"

"How about dumbstruck?"

Lucas rubbed his eyes again and gave up. He knew better than to touch his eyes, but they hurt like crazy. Straining to see in the darkness wasn't helping matters. He tried to ignore Tabitha and think of something useful to do.

"Should we turn back?" Tabitha asked.

"I don't know." Lucas kept walking.

"Would you know how to get back?"

"I don't know." Lucas got a few paces in front of her, attempting to discourage conversation. It didn't work.

"Do you know where we're going?" Tabitha put her hands on her hips and tapped her foot.

"Will ye evar stop nagging, ye wee wench?" Flatus's voice interrupted their little scuffle.

Lucas spun around, looking for the voice's source. His itchy eyes locked onto another ladder built into the wall like the one he'd surpassed via swan dive. He looked up. Flatus dangled off of the rungs with a cardboard spyglass, peering downstream in the dim sewer.

"What did you call me?" Tabitha gasped.

"Never ye mind. More important things t'discuss at the present. Like why Billy Rubin be commandeering the *Scumbucket* downstream toward open sea," Flatus said.

"Can you see it?" Lucas asked.

"Aye. I see that mutinous scum ordering about the crew like they were his own. Flog me!" Flatus swore.

"Toward open sea? Can you really sail between the sewer and the ocean?" Tabitha asked.

"Nay. The way has been sealed off, thanks to plumber villainy. But there be another way, a complicated sort o' way, but a way all the same. It jus' requires the continual truce with the plumbers t'hold up." Flatus folded the spyglass in on itself and waggled it at Lucas. It looked like two empty toilet paper tubes and a magnifying glass.

"Truce? Didn't they just attack you today?" Lucas asked.

"Aye. It be a rather fragile sort o' truce. Or non-existent. Depending on the day."

"How can you be a pirate with a plumber for a dad, Lucas?" Tabitha asked. Her words cut deep.

Lucas didn't know how to answer, and settled for a shrug.

"I wonder what that boy be playing at. Every one o' me pirates knows the delicate situation with the plumbers. There be plenty o' ways to make the situation worser betwixt us. Could be horrid, it could." Flatus climbed down off the ladder and pocketed his spyglass.

"You're telling me?" Lucas rubbed his eyes again.

"But isn't that the motto of pirates, not caring? I'd want to sail the seven seas instead of the seven sewers, personally," Tabitha said.

"What? That be blasphemy. Pirates most certainly care. Care so much fer the sea they give up the land. Give it up fer months or years on end. Give up proper food and their lady-loves. Jus' fer a breath o' salty sea air…" Flatus got lost in his thoughts. His grubby hand clapped over the mermaid tattoo on his chest.

"Uh, yeah. That pretty much explains it." Lucas didn't like the sound of years stuck anywhere, sea included. But just the same, it sounded better than breathing the rancid air in the sewer.

"We will be gettin' back there, swabs. Jus' as soon as we load up on recruits an' supplies. An' grog, o' course."

So, Flatus really was taking his crew to the open sea.

"Are you sure about this, Flatus?" Lucas asked in a whisper.

The trio of marooned pirates caught up to the *Scumbucket* as it navigated a bend in the sewer.

"See here, Puke. You'll be callin' me Cap'n, or I'll ne'er let yer scurvy-weathered, poxy self back on me crew, y'hear? An' hush up now, or we'll be caught." Flatus whispered back.

"Hypocrite," Lucas muttered. Flatus was the loudest human on the planet. How could he have the guts to tell Lucas to hush?

"I can't believe I'm stowing away on a sewer-sailing pirate ship. The plunder better be worth it, Captain... sir." Tabitha was better at this respect thing than Lucas could ever hope to be.

Flatus took his big fat gun out again. Lucas looked at it skeptically.

"Who are you going to shoot?" Tabitha asked quickly.

Flatus shot her a look.

"Captain." Tabitha corrected gracefully.

"Nobody, lass. It be a blunderbuss grappling hook, not a true pistol."

"I've had to deal with that thing before. Maybe I'd rather get shot." Lucas wrung his hands together. His stomach did a similar gesture or felt like it.

"Belay that talk, or ye'll be shark bait. Maybe that be a better name fer ye. Though ye do have a tendency to make me green under the gills, Puke." Flatus readied the gun.

Lucas was tired, and his feet were fiercely chapped. His eyes burned, and he smelled like a breath mint after his mouthwash shower. His stomach gurgled just thinking about the grappling hook. He didn't want to live up to his name, yet again.

"I make you green under the whatevers? You're the one flushing me down the toilet, flying me through the sewers, dunking me in diarrhea water, and threatening me with being eaten alive by sharks." Lucas crossed the threshold into full-on whining-mode. He wasn't proud, but the elements had gotten the best of him.

Flatus made a sound that sounded like a growl.

"Captain. Mister Captain, Sir?" Lucas yelped out all the official titles he could muster before he got hollered at again in crazy pirate-speak.

Flatus looked smug.

"Technically you dunked yourself in diarrhea water," Tabitha whispered.

"Ahh!" Lucas screamed.

"Shhh!" Flatus and Tabitha hushed him in unison.

Thunk. Lucas let his head plop back on the slimy cement wall, defeated.

Flatus pressed up against the shadows of the slimy sewer walls and motioned Tabitha and Lucas in behind him. The ship towered so far above the water level they couldn't see who was on deck. Lucas thought he saw feet pacing past some drainage openings. He pointed and poked Flatus around his generous midsection.

"I see feet. Is that where you're trying to hook the thingy? In the drain hole?" Lucas asked.

"Drain hole? That sounds like hasty-witted plumber talk. That be called a scupper, Puke."

Lucas was really tired of being cold, wet, and dirty. But he was even more tired of being thought a traitor by Flatus Codswallup.

"Look, Captain, I'm down here in the sewer with you while my Dad is going insane up top. Isn't that enough proof I'm loyal to your crew? Just because I'm grumpy doesn't mean I'm some sort of plumber traitor. I can't help who my parents are," Lucas said.

"He's right. Just like I can't help that I don't have any parents," Tabitha said.

"Awkward," Lucas muttered.

"Shut yer hawseholes," Flatus bellowed in the loudest whisper humanly possible.

"Aye-aye, Cap'n," Lucas said. His mouth stayed open, jaw lowered in disbelief. He'd actually responded properly for once. Maybe all the exhaustion and exposure to the elements had drained the punk out of him. He was pretty much too tired to care at that point, even though hawsehole sounded awfully similar to drain hole. The drive to argue had left him sometime after his pants.

"The *Scumbucket* is getting away." Tabitha flailed her hand toward it.

The ship was rounding the corner, listing hard to the right. A chunk of missing hull showed proudly above the waterline. Flatus had blamed that huge gaping hole on the siren. Lucas was skeptical about that. But Flatus was right about one thing, they did need that denture paste.

"That hole is huge — Captain," Lucas said.

"Aye... Aye," Flatus started out sadly but then perked up.

Flatus didn't wait to ask for permission. He bear-hugged Lucas and Tabitha together and launched his blunderbuss. Lucas let out a string of inappropriate remarks as they jerked violently, and his feet left the paving.

Tabitha held her breath. Lucas blacked out.

Chapter Eight

Lucas came to his senses in a smelly heap of unwashed bodies. Flatus Codswallup was underneath him, and Tabitha, with her fluorescent-orange hair, was on top. He pushed her off in the gentlest way he could manage then flopped onto the wood plank floor.

They were in a different part of the ship than Lucas had seen before. There were hammocks and bunks lining the walls and between the posts down the chamber's middle. He supposed this was where the crew slept at night.

Lucas looked over at Flatus. Unfortunately for the guys underneath him, they weren't alone in the room. By the looks of the tentacle-like dreadlocks, Crudd was stuck under the big captain. A piece of skid-marked T-shirt indicated Viscous Val, too. Lucas grabbed Flatus's arm and tugged it hard. Groans issued from the pile.

"Hush," Flatus said.

Tabitha sat on the floor with her pink-pajamaed knees tucked to her chest. Lucas didn't blame her. It was disturbing even to him. The pirates had little hygiene if any, and this bedroom was a prime example. Piles of soggy trash lined the walls, and sodden laundry hung from the rafters. It smelled worse than his P.E. teacher's armpit.

"Cap'n," Crudd jumped up and saluted once he was able. His dreadlocks swirled around him in an orange typhoon.

"What in the world? I mean, ahoy, Cap'n," Val gaped.

"At ease, crew. Keep yer voices down. An' please explain the meaning of my marooning. I'd think mutiny if yer scurvy selves had attacked just now, but as it stands, I'm rummy," Flatus said.

"Billy Rubin said ye met a sad fate. Didn't want t'believe it but had no other explanation," Crudd said.

"A sad fate? We'd been gone not more than an hour. How could he explain me sudden demise?" Flatus gestured like a crazy person.

"I didn't like the sound of it, Cap'n, but what could I do?" Crudd asked.

Val just shrugged.

Lucas wasn't impressed by their responses. The only thing more annoying than being afraid to save the captain was being the one to mutiny. Billy-stupid-Rubin.

"I'd fight fer ye, Crudd. I expect the same from yer poxy nethers too," Flatus said.

"He prolly didn't fight any too hard cuz Billy made him first mate," Val said.

"No! I mean, yes, but that be not the reason, Cap'n," Crudd shot Val a sharp look.

"Treachery at all levels. Arrr!" Flatus stormed around the cramped cabin and ripped down an empty hammock for no reason.

The *Scumbucket* made another turn in the other direction. Lucas held onto a post to steady himself. Tabitha reached out for the hull. The three pirates acted like it was no biggie and just leaned with the boat.

"Uh, guys?" Lucas pointed at the gaping hole in the hull they had come through.

A tsunami of sewer water was heading straight for them.

"Quick! Grab that keg," Lucas pointed at a huge keg that was about the same size as the hole in the hull.

Flatus looked like he wanted to argue or say something about respect, but he didn't. He reached over and grabbed the keg so easily it must have been empty. Crudd helped him, grabbing the other end. Val and Lucas ran up behind them and gave the fat part of the barrel a big shove right as the wave hit.

They were all pushed back, keg and all, but steadied themselves and shoved again, hard. A forceful spray of brown water shot in around the edges of their makeshift cork.

"Heave, ho," Crudd said.

"Aye. Heave, men. Altogether now," Flatus said.

Tabitha scurried out of her corner, avoiding the spray of foul water. She moved around the back of the keg where the other two kids were heaving and ho-ing and added her strength to the mix.

"Three, two, one, heave," Crudd called out, synchronizing their efforts.

Lucas felt wood splintering and scratching as they shoved the keg in to plug the hull hole. It wasn't a perfect fit, but it was better than letting themselves drown in sewer regurgitation. The *Scumbucket* straightened out again so the water didn't reach their level for the moment. Lucas took action in the small time they had.

"Flatus, give me the denture glue—sir." Lucas held out his hand.

"What be this, sir, nonsensicality? It be Cap'n to ye, swab," Flatus said.

"Captain of what, huh? Just give it to me." Lucas was trying, but Rome hadn't been built in a day.

"Ye fight dirty, Puke. But ye have a point. Even if we reclaim me *Scumbucket*, she won't last long with this here gaping sewer siren hole." Flatus fished in his huge pockets and handed over the tube.

"Sewer siren?" Tabitha asked.

"A vile breed of villainous sewer-spirit," Crudd explained.

"I'm not convinced on the villainous bit. She seemed pretty interesting." Lucas glopped denture glue around the bottom edge of the barrel.

"Destructive, nay interesting. This be me baby, the *Scumbucket*. I won't let her be disgraced," Flatus argued.

"I don't even get it, how she could do this. She's smaller than Tabitha," Lucas said.

"Black magic," Flatus said.

Crudd released his grip on the keg, and it stayed in place. He stuck out his hand to Tabitha. She shot him a look.

"Name's Crudd, first mate of the *Scumbucket*." Crudd wiped his hand on his pants and extended it again to Tabitha.

"Blimey, Crudd, the position means all that much to ye? I didn't rightly know, or I'd've given it to ye ages ago. I had thought yer heart still be up yonder." Flatus paced away across the cabin, apparently lost in thought. His hand found the mermaid on his chest, his thoughtful gesture.

Crudd looked away from the captain. He took a palmful of the denture glue from Lucas and started patching the topside of the keg cork. After a moment of awkward silence, Tabitha piped up again.

"I'm Tabitha. I like your hair. We could be long lost relatives." Tabitha shook her orange hair.

Crudd stared at Tabitha for a good long while before he nodded. Tabitha moved away and fussed with the patch job.

"Long lost. Could be, lass." Crudd's voice was low and mopey.

Lucas wondered where the cheery grog-gargler had disappeared to, in wake of this new grumpy Crudd. But he remembered this poor guy had had to do whatever Billy Rubin had said for the last couple hours. A fate worse than death. Coupled with a guilt trip from Flatus, Lucas figured he'd be clammed up too.

"So... sewer sirens made this hole?" Tabitha cut the tense silence.

"That's what Flatus keeps saying. I dunno, the siren I met didn't seem so threatening. I kinda liked her." Lucas wondered if Tabitha would be jealous. He kinda hoped so.

"Don't you know the legend of sirens?" Tabitha asked.

"No. I sorta thought they were what police cars have," Lucas said.

"Please tell me you're joking," Tabitha said.

"*Woowoo.*" Lucas made a police siren noise and stared at her.

"Um... yeah, no. You're wrong. They're legendary sea spirits that call to sailors. The sailors are hypnotized and go to them like zombies. And usually die in the process." Tabitha's eyes were wide and serious, like Dad got when he warned about sewer-pirates.

"Where do you get this stuff anyway?" Lucas felt himself bristling, defensive of Giardia.

"She reads," Crudd pitched in.

"Um, yeah. Yeah, I read," Tabitha said.

Lucas didn't care for the awkwardness between the two orange-haired people. He shrugged off all the siren talk and went after Flatus.

"So what's your plan for taking out that punk, Billy Rubin?" Lucas asked as he caught up to Flatus.

The captain paced back and forth along the far wall near some built-in bunks. He looked to have the weight of the world on his shoulders. He was so gloomy he didn't complain that Lucas had forgotten his title.

"Taking him out? You think we ought to... kill him?" Flatus sounded genuinely upset about it.

"Um, yeah. Or I guess if you're chicken you could just maroon him like he did to you, right?" Didn't pirates kill people? Wasn't that the point of it all?

"He may be a punk like ye say, but I took him under me wing an' now..." Flatus gulped air.

"Are you okay?" Lucas asked.

If Flatus cried, Lucas would have to try pretty hard not to laugh at him. This was not appropriately tough pirate behavior. Well, if he had learned anything from his little sister Chelsea, sometimes people just needed someone to blame. Lucas was used to being the scapegoat around the house, and he supposed he could give it a go here as well.

"I'll do it. So you don't have to," Lucas said.

"Do… it?" Flatus was painfully naïve for a pirate.

"I will get rid of him." Lucas said it slowly, like talking to Chelsea to make her feel dumb.

Lucas was pretty sure he didn't want to kill Billy, despite hating him. But he'd laugh his butt off if he could throw him overboard. In that pretty brocade coat. All covered in poo-juice. Yes, he'd enjoy that a whole lot.

Flatus looked at him, thinking. Lucas stared back; Flatus wasn't too goofy at the moment, just serious and depressed. Lucas figured he might also be serious and depressed if his ship and crew got mutinied away from him in the course of an hour. But not all the crew had flopped. Crudd and Val still seemed savvy.

"You can't take back the ship with yourself alone, Flatus."

"Aye."

Flatus still didn't argue about not being called captain. That made Lucas feel yucky and depressed for him. He had to get the goofy old confident Flatus back before he washed his hands, literally, of all this piracy stuff.

"Crudd is on your side. Just promise him the first mate job once Billy Rubin's done for, and you'll have someone to fight for you. Val might like moving up in the ranks too. How about the cook?" Lucas had learned a thing or two from playing shoot-em-up video games. Pirating was a team game; party numbers were needed to survive.

"Aye! Good thought, Puke, I'll go talk smartly to Crudd right now. Ye can discuss the overthrow with Viscous Val there, aye?"

Lucas turned and saw Val standing way too close to Tabitha. And surprisingly, Lucas cared.

"Can you give me any tips to survive... this?" Tabitha asked Viscous Val.

Lucas frowned. He wasn't really buddies with Tabitha in the real world, but down here, she was the closest thing he had to a friend. She was the reason he'd gotten himself all slathered with gooey sewer chunks. The reason he'd come back at all. Lucas was almost free from this stinky old privy-pirate life.

"Yeah I'm full of tips, girl. Take this." Val handed her a spray bottle of bleach, not unlike the one Lucas had lost during his headfirst sewer dive.

"Thanks." Tabitha held it like a two-handed axe across her chest.

Lucas burped to announce his presence. *Urrrrrp.*

"Ahh!" Tabitha might have complained about the rudeness back home. But here, she stayed quiet. She knew better now; a burp wasn't much to whine about. Lucas grinned widely at her. She frowned but wasn't scared off.

"The spray bottle might help a tiny bit, but do you have anything sharp to defend yourself with?" Lucas asked.

"As if." Tabitha made an exasperated sigh. She lifted her arms to display her pink-pajamafied body. Point taken. She was as soft and fluffy as a cotton ball.

"That's okay, I'll look out for you." Lucas stood a bit taller. He tried to think of Tabitha as his own little sister.

"Thanks, I think..." Tabitha looked skeptical.

Val laughed loudly until he snorted. Lucas raised his eyebrow at him. He wasn't impressed by Val and was quickly learning to hate him. His protective instinct kicked in.

"Relax, Val, I've got this." Lucas put his hand on Val's shoulder.

"You've got this? You've got—" Val laughed so hard he doubled over.

Viscous Val's laughing turned to coughing, and he spat onto the wooden plank floor. Lucas cringed away, dodging with his bare feet. He side stepped in front of Tabitha who made an appreciative noise. Lucas hadn't meant to be chivalrous, but it seemed to turn out that way.

"Protecting her from my spit won't help squat, Puke. We gotta toughen her up a bit to survive this crew," Val said.

Tabitha looked herself over. Could she get any girlier? Lucas hoped it wasn't contagious. And better yet, hopefully it was curable.

"But anyway, don't worry. We can go back at some point. That guy with the dreadlocks over there said he came on adventures and went home after all of 'em. He was like, really into it, so now he's permanent," Lucas said.

"How could anybody be really into this? We're in the sewer," Tabitha said the word sewer like it was a curse.

"Maybe the plunder's decent?" Lucas suggested.

"We're all really into it. Much better than sitting at home watching TV and being ignored by my dad. Or worse, not being ignored by my dad." Val gave Lucas and Tabitha a purposeful look.

Lucas looked back at him. Val apparently had issues. Lucas made a mental note to assume people had issues and not be so mean to them. The meanest people usually had the most problems.

"Well, at least you have a dad." Tabitha tried to be polite.

"Meh. Sailing is great, anyway. I love ships, and soon we'll get our rumps back into the open sea like real pirates. We are real pirates. Cap'n has just got some kinks to iron out between him and the plumbers," Val said.

"Ah, the plumbers..." Lucas rubbed his temples.

"Yeah, I dunno much about it, but Cap'n says there used to be a truce between the plumbers and pirates. There used to be free passage between the real open sea and the sewers. That's why he's recruiting more jerks like you. Trying to patch up the *Scumbucket*. To get back there. To wherever the real sea-pirates are. And where his girlfriend is," Val said.

"Recruiting jerks like you, too." Tabitha pointed at Val.

Lucas grinned and gave her a high five. She reluctantly accepted the hand slap. Lucas didn't blame her for the reluctance; his hands were covered in every filth known to man.

"Who asked you, lady? Anyway, that's why I didn't run Billy right through when he said the Cap'n was gone and he was taking us out to open sea. Who wants to stay in here when the real ocean's just chillin' out there, waiting for us?" Viscous Val seemed authentic.

Lucas still didn't forgive him for marooning Flatus along with the rest of the crew. But there was still time to repent.

"How old is the dude, anyway? Flatus can't be much older than Dad, but he looks a bit more... weathered." Lucas scratched his head.

"I dunno," Val said.

"And whaddya mean, his girlfriend?" Lucas asked.

"Y'know, that mermaid chick. The one on his tattoo and on the front of the ship." Val acted annoyed, like it was obvious.

"Oh." Lucas looked over toward Flatus and Crudd and saw them deep in discussion.

"Mermaids are... real?" Tabitha asked.

"I guess, but I've never seen one. Yo, ho, yo, ho... a pirate's life for me." Val made a dorky pirate gesture and did a jig.

Despite the general grossness, sailing wasn't half-bad. So long as Lucas got to shower afterward. Being on staff permanently sounded impossible—having to go to sleep without a proper shower? Yuck! But Val seemed perfectly content underneath his layer of slime. To each their own.

Lucas wondered if someday he'd get to sail something clean with fresh air blowing about him. On the ocean, under the sun, with sweet-salty sea air. Ahh, he could see it now. Well, it wasn't going to happen on the *Scumbucket* as long as Billy Rubin was in power. The jerk couldn't keep peace among his crew, let alone make a truce with the plumbers.

"So about those tips you wanted. Don't lean over the railing too far. Watch out for the alligators." Val turned his body toward Tabitha to exclude Lucas from the conversation.

"There are alligators in the sewers?" Tabitha looked a little uneasy.

"You told me there weren't any alligators in the sewers," Lucas butted in and stuck his finger in Val's chest.

"I never said any such thing. I said there weren't any crocodiles in the sewers," Val said.

"What? Gimme a break," Lucas groaned and flailed his hands with annoyance.

"You don't know anything about the sewers. You're just a noob," Val said, his voice escalating.

"Whatever," Lucas couldn't even get to the point of things with this moron.

"Don't trust that loser. When the time comes, I'll watch out for ya, girly." Val struck a pose and smiled.

Tabitha looked back and forth between Lucas and Val. Weighing her options?

Why did Lucas care what she chose? Because he'd jumped into the manhole for her, he figured. He was going to protect her, even if only to make himself feel better.

"Hey. Back off. There's more important things to fight about right now. Like getting Captain Flatus's boat back." Lucas stepped between Tabitha and Val.

"Alligators and crocodiles aren't the same thing. Not nearly. When you need someone to fight for you, pick someone who's not dumb." Val's eyes flickered pointedly between Tabitha and Lucas.

Lucas held his tongue. Viscous Val was trying to make trouble. He didn't really even care if Tabitha liked Val more than him, so why fight?

Val watched him like a hawk, waiting to strike on any wrong move.

Lucas shrugged, and Val looked furious.

"And anyway, why would I want to help that lout? Billy Rubin promised me and the rest of the crew open ocean. We're headed there now." Val scowled at Lucas, waiting for a reaction.

"You mean to drain the sewers into the ocean?" Tabitha looked horrified.

It sounded pretty gross to Lucas too, but it couldn't be more damaging than an oil spill, right? He wondered if Tabitha knew more about this environmental protection stuff than he did, but didn't ask. He didn't want Val to see any show of weakness.

"It'll happen whether we try stopping it or not. Just wait. And when the time comes, girly-girl, just ask." Val leered at her like a creeper. Lucas gagged.

Suddenly the *Scumbucket* lurched like someone had slammed on the brakes. Lucas fell backward on his rump and grabbed for the hem of his pillowcase to shield his dignity. Tabitha found a post and grabbed on for dear life. Val bent his knees, crouched, and managed to stay upright with a bit of hopping and shuffling.

Oh no. What was happening now? Could it possibly get any worse?

"We be under attack," Flatus's voice pierced their tension.

It had gotten worse.

Chapter Nine

"Hurtin' hemorrhoids!" Viscous Val sprinted up and out of the cabin. He apparently had somewhere better to be.

Lucas was half-glad to see him go, because he didn't trust him as far as he could throw him. The other half was worried he was taking off, because he'd blow their cover.

"Puke— It be yer time to shine, lad. Ye said ye'd take care o' that festering carbuncle Billy. I be countin' on ye. I'll take Crudd and gather the rest o' the crew an' back ye up. But if it goes badly fer me, then it's all on yer shoulders, matey." Flatus put his big hand on Lucas's shoulder.

"Aye-aye, captain." Lucas gained two inches of height when the heavy hand lifted. Despite Flatus's bumbling good-nature, he could be pretty tough if he tried with a grip like that.

"Sorry I called ye a plumber, mate," Flatus said.

Lucas smiled, glad for the moment he wasn't ditched as a plumber insurgent. The feeling might change if he died or plunged into sewer water again. Or if he actually wound up, ugh, killing Billy. Throwing him overboard would be all toots and giggles, but running him through? Lucas's stomach churned.

Flatus gave Crudd a shove on the shoulder, and they headed toward the galley. Maybe old Thumper, the one-legged cook, would be on their side. Hopefully he was better in a fight than he was in the kitchen. Actually, rat jerky might be deadly. That could be useful.

Tabitha seemed ready to spray anyone who came near her with the spray bottle Val had given her. She looked much fiercer than Lucas ever had, when faced with a dirty toilet bowl, anyway. He scooped the air to call her over. She nodded, and they headed up to the main deck.

At first, Lucas was scared to be seen. Wouldn't the crew be alerted that the marooning hadn't gone as planned? Nope. There was so much chaos on deck that he could have arrived dressed as a giant chicken and not raised any eyebrows. He stuck out his arm and stopped Tabitha getting run over by battle-crazed pirates.

Lucas scanned the random pirate insanity. Billy Rubin was dressed up in his fancy, ruffled pirate attire, the polar opposite of everyone else on the crew. Lucas saw him across the bustling ship because he had perched high on the poop deck. He waggled a shiny new blade over the railing. He looked like an overdressed, shrunken dictator.

Lucas tried to get a sense of what was causing all the panic but couldn't see anything besides a yelling Billy and some scrambling pirates.

"That chump up there in the fancy coat is Billy Rubin. I've got to take him out." Lucas pointed.

"Take him out? To dinner?" Tabitha gave Lucas a look like she knew what he meant but didn't like it. He wasn't sure whether to correct her, laugh, or ignore her.

The decision was forgotten with a bizarre loud noise, like something on the Titanic movie. *Braaaaaaw.*

That couldn't be good. Lucas's heart stopped, listening to it. It sounded like a tree in a windstorm, groaning and cracking. Or like a whale speaking. Uh-oh.

Lucas finally had the sense to look up. The sewer snake was back. Ahem, the kraken, if fairytales were preferred to reality. Now it was equipped with three tentacle arms, all latched onto various parts of the *Scumbucket*. The thickest strongest one gripped tightly on the main mast. Unfortunately for the mast, it wasn't very flexible. Right at the midsection, it bent way too far for something made of solid wood. It cracked loudly like air bubble packaging. It was going to snap!

"Good gravies," Lucas grabbed Tabitha's hand. He wasn't sure where he'd lead them, but anywhere was better than directly underneath the cracking mast. Under the poop deck in the captain's cabin seemed a decent hideout. Unfortunately, it meant running right in front of Billy Rubin as he leered over the railing.

"Kraken!" Billy Rubin's voice sounded over the chaos as they got closer. The mast looked like it might hold—it was still groaning but hadn't snapped like a twig, yet. Unfortunately for the crew, their new captain wasn't doing anything useful to brace it besides yelling obvious stuff.

"Thank you, Captain Obvious," Lucas yelled at him. The plumber's tentacle was latched onto the mast for several minutes already. What good was announcing its arrival going to do?

"That's Captain Rubin, swab," Billy yelled and pointed his blade toward Lucas.

Lucas ignored him and kept moving toward the captain's cabin, Tabitha in tow.

"Where do you think... hey! Stop that. That is my official captain's office," Billy yelled.

Lucas ignored him and opened the outhouse door marked *W.C.* He pushed Tabitha toward the door, and she didn't question him. Lucas stepped back and threw caution to the wind.

"This is not your office, and you're not the captain. This is Flatus's cabin, and you are nothing but a whiny chump, who couldn't become a captain without tricks." Lucas hollered.

Billy didn't look very threatening. In fact, he had gone a bit white. Ha! He knew he wasn't even tough enough to beat a kid.

Snowflakes of shredded toilet-paper sails floated down over them as a gust of warm and fetid air blew through the sewer. Lucas remembered he wasn't wearing any pants when his undercarriage felt the breeze, and his pillowcase fluttered.

Lucas's lips curled in a smile as he plotted his next move. He spun around, bent over, and flipped up the back of his makeshift tunic. He hadn't had a good opportunity to moon someone in way too long.

"Nyah, nyah," Lucas wiggled his butt back and forth.

"Attack. Attack! For the love of the sea, *attack*," Billy yelled.

Something stomped around the deck. Was the crew really going to come and attack him just for mooning that punk Billy? The world wasn't a fair place, pirate ships included.

"That's a bit harsh eh? Can't handle being mooned?" Lucas stood up and covered himself.

Directly in front of him was a huge man. He was as tall as Flatus and twice as fat. He looked like he could squash Lucas underneath his big work boot.

Apparently, it wasn't Lucas who needed attacking.

"Ahhh!" Lucas screamed. Who was this gargantuan man-beast? He whirled around without a second look and made a beeline for anywhere besides there.

The man's huge hand easily reached out and latched onto Lucas's shoulder. He yelped and lunged for the captain's cabin door. A couple of his fingers hooked through the cutout moon shape on the door. The big dude basically picked him up and started pulling. Lucas's fingers ached, but he was too afraid to let go.

"Lucas," Tabitha said from inside the door.

"Uh, hi?" Lucas choked out between screaming for his life.

"Are you okay?" Tabitha asked.

Lucas's fingers absorbed some splinters from the door. He tried to get a better grip but didn't have much luck. His hands burned.

"Do I look okay?" Lucas said.

"Isn't that your dad?" Tabitha asked.

"What? No. Why in the world—" Lucas said.

Lucas whipped his head around to investigate before his fingers broke. Why would Tabitha think this huge monster guy was Dad? Oh. He was decked out in the dorky Viking Plumbers' attire, of course.

Once Lucas stopped struggling, the guy let him loose. He had that same trucker's hat with fake horns that said Viking Plumbers. The shirt was the same too, like it was recycled from a retro-bowling league. The nametag read *Simon*. Lucas didn't completely remember this guy, but the name did ring a bell. And his bald head with the fat black moustache did look kinda familiar.

"Uh, hey, Simon," Lucas said.

"Yo. You da Goodspeed kid, yeah?" Simon asked.

"Yeah. Did Dad send you after me?" Lucas had transitioned through most emotions in the last minute and a half, but was currently embarrassed. Dad couldn't shimmy on down a sewer snake to rescue him, and instead had sent this hulking beast Simon?

"Yeah, he—" Simon couldn't get out the last of the words because Billy Rubin stabbed him in the thigh with a makeshift sewer blade.

Simon grunted. He kicked his thick leg and sent Billy scuffling away on his shiny buckled boots. After a few steps, Billy found some mucous on the deck and slipped. Lucas let out a loud guffaw as he watched the first mate bite it.

The other pirates hanging around suddenly backed off when they saw Simon own Billy like that. Billy struggled to untangle himself from his extra ruffles and Simon didn't even acknowledge he had been stabbed.

"Are you okay, dude?" Lucas asked him.

"Yeah, jus' a scratch, kid." Simon shrugged as the thigh of his khakis turned dark with blood. Lucas wasn't so sure it was just a scratch, but he didn't want to argue with the guy. He wondered if Flatus had plundered any antiseptics today.

"That's hardcore," Lucas said, and he meant it. If he had gotten a paper cut down there, he'd be hollering like a banshee and imagining all the most horrible strains of *E. coli* getting under his skin.

"Now c'mere you. Yer pop's worried sick. Let's go before I go an' get stabbed again." Simon grinned under his moustache.

"Why didn't he come for me himself?" Lucas dropped his voice.

"He'll be here any minute, him and the rest of the after-hours plumbers. But I'd rather just haul you up an' out of 'ere without any more... complications."

"Hey, mister, I don't blame you. But I got a score to settle here with this punk." Lucas pointed at Billy Rubin.

"Come to think of it, I've got a score to settle with 'im too." Simon eyed Billy hungrily.

Billy trembled, and his crotch area darkened.

Lucas laughed.

"If ye got a score t'settle wit'im, ye got a score t'settle wit' me," a phlegm-choked voice hollered from behind Simon and Lucas.

"Huh?" Lucas whirled around and saw the oldest matey onboard.

He was a wrinkly guy who sounded like he needed to hock up the biggest loogie in the history of loogies. He was wearing basically the same outfit as Lucas, a sack-shaped tunic, but with short pants underneath. He had an eyepatch over one of his sunken eye sockets.

"He may be a whimperin' blimey fool of a lad barely grown out o' his poxy pimples, but he be the rightful cap'n since Cap'n Codswallup met Davy Jones," the old dude said.

"Thanks, Chummy." Billy took his head out of his ruffled rump and proved completely oblivious to the thinly veiled insult. He stood up and tried to brush himself off.

"It's a lie!" Lucas yelled. Flatus didn't die. Who would believe this dude? Ugh.

"What be a lie, Puke?" Chummy asked. He wielded a long copper blade that looked like a filed-down chunk of piping. He held it toward the deck, not threatening Lucas quite yet, but at the ready. Maybe it was because of his new huge plumber friend Simon who stood like a silent shadow, waiting to see how things unfolded.

"All of it. Billy Rubin is a liar! Flatus is not dead. Billy marooned him, and me," Lucas said.

"Don't listen to him. Run him through, Chummy. Flay him! Make him walk the plank," Billy's voice rose higher like the whiner he was.

"Don't be listenin' t'im 'cause he be a liar, or 'cause yer a liar?" Chummy narrowed his wrinkled eye and looked back and forth between Billy and Lucas.

"He is," Lucas and Billy said at the same time, pointing at the other.

"An' since when does dis crew flay? Since when does we run 'em through? Verges on barbaric, me-thinks. A nice swim, or a good case o' runs be pun-ishment enough. Fer even the most festering of car-buncles." Chummy twirled his shining blade thought-fully.

"And I've already walked the plank today. Don't care for another swim, thanks." Lucas didn't know what flaying was, but he would most certainly like to avoid being run through. Especially run through with something used to clean toilets.

"Your pirate law is your own business. But the kid ain't walking no planks. He's wit' me." Simon put his bulk between Lucas and the pirates. Lucas tried to peer around him to see what was happening but failed. He settled for crouching down to watch from between Simon's knees.

"Plumber scum," some pirate called out. The group thickened. Flatus's job rallying the crew to his side wasn't going so well, so far as Lucas could see. Lucas swallowed a lump in his throat.

"Aye! Get the plumber," Billy Rubin sensed his chance to divert attention away from himself and grabbed on with both hands.

"Get t'safety, kid. Time to clear out this cesspool," Simon said.

What? This wasn't supposed to be happening. The pirates were supposed to be on his side against that annoying Billy Rubin. Where was Flatus Codswallup? Had something gone wrong? Had the cook knocked him out because he preferred Billy as captain? Had he gone to meet Davy Jones in truth? Lucas felt nauseous. The adrenaline that fueled him to confront Billy was drained. His aches and pains were noticeable again. His feet hurt. His eyes burned. His stomach rolled.

And just when it couldn't get any worse… a thunderous sound split the sewer air. *Crrraaack.*

The *Scumbucket's* mast snapped clean in two.

Pressure, caused by the flowing sewer water, pulled against the kraken-caught mast until it buckled. All labels were forgotten when the *Scumbucket* gave way. The flying telephone-pole-sized log did not discriminate whether its victim was a pirate of Billy's, a pirate of Flatus's, or a plumber. Lucas's ears rang with the massive snap, and he fell to the filthy planks as the ship lurched. It wasn't a moment too soon. The severed mast swooped over the deck like a fishhook on the end of a wildly cast line.

"Ahh!" Simon cried as some part of him got walloped by the flying mast. He was a bulky man, but the force brought him down face-first.

"Eeeek!" Pirates screamed.

Lucas lay on deck, wishing he could dissolve into the planks. Flying splinters from the cracking mast flew like shrapnel and took people down better than the makeshift cutlasses the pirates wielded.

The massive ship twirled, no longer tethered by the sewer snake, facing forward into the path of least resistance. Lucas rolled down the sloping deck toward the captain's cabin. *Thunk. Thunk. Thunk.* His head hit the planks without cushion. His stomach was a damp towel being wrung out and he dry heaved.

"Lucas?" Tabitha's voice found Lucas's swirling brain.

"Huh?" Lucas groaned. The ship leveled out and resumed drifting peacefully down the sewer pipe. He face-planted into the W.C. cabin door.

"What's happening? I can't get the door open," Tabitha said.

"I'm a pretty good doorstop, yeah?" Lucas tried for a pitiful joke.

"Yarr! Me ship? What happened to me ship?" Flatus's voice cut through the crew's caterwauling.

Lucas rolled over and saw the captain burst up from below decks with a handful of pirates at his back. He had a different weapon now, some sort of towel bar filed to a point at one end. His timing was pretty good for himself, but pretty lousy for Lucas. He groaned.

"Captain." Billy Rubin stood up and straightened his coat. Apparently Billy hadn't been killed in the chaos. Shucks.

"Uh-oh, kid. Might be we're not getting any backup, now." Simon lifted his face off the deck and gruffly whispered to Lucas. No!

Lucas watched the kraken clutching the main mast like an oversized fishing pole out in the murky sewer water. The Jolly Plunger flag got soggy and sank. Gobs of wet toilet-paper sails scattered and floated around like tiny icebergs around the Titanic. If that sewer snake was the way Simon had shimmied down onto the *Scumbucket*, no other plumbers could follow. The path was a one-way ticket to sewer dipping. He'd been there, done that, would need antibiotics later, thanks to his little dive. He gave a helpless shrug at Simon.

Lucas tried to melt into the wall and let Flatus and Billy fight it out. If Flatus won, the plumbers wouldn't need backup anyway. If Billy won... well, Lucas might be inspired to take one more dip into the sewer sludge. Better to walk the plank than be keel-hauled; he didn't know what filthy barnacles grew on the ship's hull.

Billy and Flatus were actually discussing something in a partially civilized way. They spoke face to face, but their voices were rising. They both looked red, and neither was happy. Lucas wondered when it'd come to blows.

Sewer water splashed around the *Scumbucket*, noisier than usual. This portion of the pipes moved faster than the stagnant waters upstream. Lucas wondered where they were headed and if anyone was steering.

Steering... on the poop deck. Lucas started to laugh, but was cut short by the clang of metal on metal. Flatus and Billy were dueling.

"Yar — Avast! En garde." Those and other piratey expletives were slung around the deck of the *Scumbucket* like ammunition.

Flatus rallied up nearly half the crew, but some of the idiot pirates were still standing by Billy Rubin's side. Others were downed. Whether by flying mast shards or being run through by plunger cutlasses, Lucas couldn't tell.

"Let me out of here," Tabitha thumped on the opposite side of the captain's cabin door.

Lucas tried standing but was still dizzy and nauseated. He crawled a couple feet away, and Tabitha burst out of the door with a fury that didn't match her ruffled pink pajamas. She had an armload of weapons and tossed one at Lucas.

"Yowch." Lucas fumbled and cut himself on a rather sharp, broken, hand mirror. It seemed like a purposeful break, transforming the froufrou fancy mirror into a slashing knife-like weapon. He spun it around and cut through the air to test it out.

Tabitha went to Simon's side and pulled him off the deck. In truth, he did most of the work with standing, but she thrust a weapon into his hands. It was a sharpened plunger similar to what Flatus had wielded earlier, but it was made out of plastic. The tip shone even in the dim light, razor-sharp and jagged. Simon grabbed it down around the rubber suctiony part and got a feel for it. Lucas watched, hoping he didn't fight like a dairy farmer.

Tabitha dual-wielded the bleach spray Val had given her earlier and a can of tub-scrubbing foam. She looked like a fluffy pink ninja, even more eager to fight than Lucas.

The dueling was contagious; more battles sprung up around them on all sides. Lucas waved his weapon, trying to look menacing. A couple pirates engaged Simon, and he pushed them back with his plunger blade.

Tabitha dodged a swinging cutlass and strode right up to where Billy Rubin and Flatus Codswallup exchanged blows. Lucas scampered after her, partly to get away from the fight Simon the plumber had found. The entire mess was too confusing. They needed jerseys so Lucas could tell who was on whose team. Right now, all he knew was that Flatus needed backup. He wouldn't let that slimy rascal Billy Rubin win. Never.

Clink. Clang. Ting. Ping. The two would-be captains dueled just like real pirates, despite their sewer-style blades.

"Just surrender, Billy. Flatus is the true captain," Lucas encouraged from a safe distance.

Tabitha threw caution to the wind and edged up behind Billy with her cleaning products. Lucas cringed and waited, silently cursing himself for not being as brave as Tabitha. He closed his eyes tight and took a deep breath. He'd rush Billy from one side while Flatus and Tabitha closed him in on the others. Yes, that would be brave and not terribly stupid.

"Arrr!" Lucas hollered a battle cry and leaped.

He never got off the ground. Lucas ended up on his back with a pair of grimy hands around his neck. The mirror blade dropped out of his fingers and clattered beside him.

Lucas looked up into Chummy's weathered and one-eyed face. He wasn't saying anything as he choked the life out of Lucas, due to the cutlass clamped between his teeth. Surprisingly, his teeth were pearly white and his breath was minty fresh as he growled. If he survived this, Lucas would have to start gargling grog more often. It worked wonders, even on sewer-sailors.

"Do you know—" Lucas spat out the words, despite being strangled.

"Grrr," Chummy replied.

"—where that cutlass has been?" Lucas choked out a laugh. Even if he died right then, he'd die with a smile on his face, watching this old dude eat plunger-scum.

At first Lucas thought his statement had fallen on deaf ears. Chummy kept his full weight on Lucas, pressing the breath out of his lungs with his knees. Stars flickered across Lucas's vision. He stretched his fingers farther than natural in an attempt to recover his blade. It had slid out of reach on a patch of mucousy filth. Lucas flailed and pounded the deck. His heart raced now; this death thing seemed real. He wasn't smiling anymore.

"Yarrrgh!" Chummy suddenly fell over backward and released Lucas from his grip. His cutlass clattered onto the deck, and he abandoned it freely. It looked like Chummy had seen a ghost.

And maybe he had. The siren had returned. And she was right next to Tabitha.

"Tab," Lucas sputtered. His throat felt like he'd gargled drain de-clogger after Chummy had nearly murdered him.

121

Tabitha sprayed bleach all over Billy Rubin. He whined about the loss of his coat's luster while parrying Flatus's thrusts with his blade. She looked up mid-squirt at Lucas when he called her. She looked meaner than a hippo with a hernia.

"Did I say you could call me Tab?"

"Watch out," Lucas croaked. He pointed at the wispy shadow of a siren looming over her shoulder. Was that Giardia? Or was there more than one siren floating about? Lucas wasn't sure whether she was dangerous or not. He wasn't going to believe that sewer sirens were evil just because some bumbling pirate had said so. And maybe, just a little bit, Lucas wanted Giardia for himself.

Tabitha sprayed some foaming cleanser at Billy's black buckled shoes before bothering to turn around. But when she did, the hypnosis was instant. She looked like a sleepwalking zombie, willing to follow the siren to wherever it wanted.

"No!" Lucas yelled in frustration, hurting his throat.

He looked over to Simon the plumber, who was busy planting his fist into the faces of the pirates and parrying their sword thrusts. Unfortunately, even Flatus's allies saw the plumber as the devil himself and attacked him generously. Simon's fist didn't discriminate either; any pirate was a good punching bag. Here was yet another reason jerseys would be helpful. Footballers couldn't be expected to tackle the right guy unless his outfit was different, right?

Lucas looked around helplessly. Who could help Tabitha now? Lucas couldn't do this alone. What could he do? Tackle the siren? She seemed transparent, like he'd just go right through her. Tackle Tabitha? That'd be pretty fun, but might not help anything if the siren was still looming and ended up hypnotizing them both.

Lucas wasn't sure why he didn't want to frolic off into the sunset with the siren at the moment, but he seized the opportunity. He stood up and grabbed his blade, careful to grip the blunt end. He wondered if maybe a blade could slice a siren, and there was only one way to find out. He swallowed hard, still unsure if he wanted to kill Giardia. She seemed so nice…

"Avast, ye scurvy swab. I groomed yer cankered rump t'be me replacement when I was dead an' gone, not a minute before that—Ye deceitful, pompous, pimply rascal," Flatus yelled and swatted Billy hard with the blunt of his cutlass.

"Oh," Billy squealed and backpedaled. He stepped in the patch of foam Tabitha had laid for him and fell hard, right in front of Lucas. Lucas tripped over his ruffled coat and went down too, clacking his teeth as his chin hit the deck.

"Unghf." Lucas's mirror-blade hit the deck and shattered into a thousand tiny bits of reflective glass. Oh, wonderful. Seven years of bad luck in addition to all this insanity.

"Puke," someone said. Lucas's ears rang, and he forgot what he was trying to do, but he managed to turn his head. He saw the orange dreadlocks that could only belong to Crudd.

"Buh?" Lucas asked. Crudd reached down and grabbed his hand. Lucas flew off the deck with the lean pirate's surprising strength.

"Watch the glass, Puke," Crudd said.

Lucas nodded, and his brain sloshed in his skull. He groaned.

"We gotta save Tabitha," Lucas said. Tabitha was the priority. He repeated the thought in his mind, trying to convince himself.

"Blasted bare feet," Crudd cried out. They couldn't walk right over and save her because of the glass.

"Siren scum," Flatus Codswallup wore boots and crunched right over the mirror shards.

The siren moved more quickly than a giant pirate in boots and clasped Tabitha's hand in her dark wispy whatever-they-were. She smiled a shadow-smile and urged Tabitha onto the railing of the *Scumbucket*. Tabitha did, without hesitation. Her eyes were blank, and her mouth was ajar.

Flatus froze, afraid to get any closer in fear of them jumping.

Lucas had a stupid idea. "Take me instead," he said.

Time stood still after Lucas offered himself up to the siren. It seemed like everyone on deck stopped their swashbuckling, spun their heads around, and looked at Lucas. He felt pretty dumb for a second there.

The siren stared at Lucas, despite lack of eyes, and he stared back. It was definitely the same siren from earlier, Giardia, from the magical undersea land of Ascaris. She apparently had no feet, as Lucas could finally see as she stood up on the ship's railing. The siren was some mix of the Grim Reaper and a floating childlike mermaid. In a word: freaky. In two words: epically awesome. The awkward moment snapped when the siren responded.

"Lucas. You've become one of them..." Giardia had a sorrowful echo in her voice.

"Says who?" Lucas's voice raised an octave, and he cleared his throat. His mind clouded, and he wanted to say anything to look better to Giardia. Even renounce his status on the *Scumbucket's* crew.

"Says you, that be who." Flatus looked at him sternly.

"Shut your trap, Flatus. I'm trying to save Tabitha," Lucas complained.

Flatus shut his trap, but didn't look happy about it.

Lucas would worry later whether he was ruining his chances at becoming a career pirate. Respect just didn't come easily to him, especially when the enemy of the pirate captain was so enchanting. And anyway, he had higher priorities. Like the life of his not-quite-friend, Tabitha. And whether he was going overboard with Giardia.

"So anyway, let her go and take me instead," Lucas reiterated.

"I don't want you anymore, Lucas. Tabitha will make a lovely siren," Giardia said.

Lucas went white. He felt a bit offended. Then a bit grateful. Then a bit scared out of his mind for Tabitha. She wasn't just going to get kidnapped; she was going to get murdered or mutilated or sirenified.

"Nuh-uh," Lucas didn't even convince himself with his objection, but at least he'd made one. The rest of the crew looked as unmoving as cave paintings. Besides one pirate. Lucas caught a flash of orange out of the corner of his eye. Crudd!

"Keep talking," Crudd muttered as he crept past Lucas. His rat stared at Lucas from his shoulder, but it kept quiet. It was too smart for a rat, really. Even Lucas couldn't be quiet when he should.

"Why can't I be a siren?" Lucas asked without thinking. He had a knack for speaking before thinking.

"You're a boy. Sirens are girls," Giardia said.

"What, are you sexist?" Lucas tried to sound offended as he pulled out one of Tabitha's earlier remarks. It had worked against Lucas when she'd accused him of it, anyway. He also tried to keep his eyes off of the creeping dreadlocked pirate who was proving to be one tough cookie. He walked right over the shattered mirror shards in bare feet without saying a word. What a good dude, helping Tabitha.

"What does sexist mean?" Giardia asked.

"It means you're discriminating against me based on my gender. That's illegal." Lucas pulled some serious-sounding stuff out of his butt that may or may not have applied to the situation.

He figured sewer sirens weren't legal citizens of the United States of America, nor did they pay taxes, nor did laws apply to them. If any species was all-female naturally, they couldn't have sexism, right? Or could they? Lucas's head hurt. Probably not quite as bad as Crudd's feet hurt. He'd left a red trail behind him as his cut feet bled over the germ-infested *Scumbucket*.

"I wanted you for a friend. I want Tabitha for an apprentice. That is more important, Lucas." Giardia stared into Lucas's face. Her voice sounded sweet and smoky. Lucas faded into la-la land, as if the siren had just flipped a switch and turned on her hypnosis. What a neat thing, a siren. A real live siren... How lovely she was. And such a pretty name, Giardia. Lucas took a step forward toward her. A step toward Ascaris...

His bare foot implanted itself into the spray of broken-glass shards from his hand-mirror cutlass. Lucas snapped out of it as quickly as he'd sunk into the hypnotic siren spell.

"Yeeoowww!" Lucas wailed and clutched his foot.

Giardia dropped Tabitha's hand and reached toward Lucas in his agony.

"Get yer hands off me daughter," Crudd yelled. He stopped creeping and charged toward the siren at full speed.

Lucas let his jaw drop. Daughter? He knew it. He should have known from the first time he'd seen that electric orange mop of messy hair on Crudd that he was related to Tabitha. He'd asked her where her parents were before, but never thought he'd figure it out on his own.

"Daughter?" Flatus crowed. The sentiment echoed through the crew. Surprise. Confusion. Horror. That their good mate, Crudd, had a daughter whose existence was threatened by the pesky sewer siren that plagued them all.

Lucas wasn't sure what to expect when Crudd collided with the siren. He half-expected him to sail right through her. But then again, he'd seen Tabitha holding her hand before. Giardia didn't follow normal rules in any sense. Anything could happen.

Crudd football-tackled the sewer siren like a pro. The siren got owned, just like a real person. She must have been really light and airy though, because Crudd kept moving as though he hadn't hit anything. Until he hit the railing—he hit that plenty hard.

"Ahh!" Tabitha yelled. The railing shook when Crudd hit it. Tabitha lost her balance, teetered precariously, and fell onto the deck. Phew, that was the safer direction to fall.

Crudd was a lean pirate with wiry strength, but he fell the other direction. The worse direction. The overboard direction. He clung onto the railing longer than the average pirate could have, but gravity was against him. He dangled over the rancid sewer water by half a hand.

"Tabitha, Honey Bear..." Crudd strained to look at his daughter between the rails. The fat sewer rat on his shoulder squealed and managed to climb up his dreadlocks like rope to save itself. It flopped awkwardly over the railing and disappeared into the chaos on deck.

"No." Tabitha's face was blank. Remnants of siren hypnosis? Maybe she just didn't care about her dear old dad. He certainly hadn't been part of her life. She tucked her pink pajama-clad knees into her chest and formed a protective ball. She didn't make eye contact with Crudd, as he dangled by a thread.

Lucas wanted to help, but he wasn't sure how. He tried to put his foot down again, but it found more shards of glass, and he whimpered, annoyed and unable to do anything.

Where had the siren gone? Lucas was still here, and so was Tabitha, but that shadowy girl-creature had *poofed*. Had it really given up that easily and taken off without an apprentice or a friend?

"It's me, Honey Bear. It's Daddy." Time stood still as Crudd begged for a word from Tabitha before he met his fate.

"No," Tabitha said again.

Lucas didn't blame her for being skeptical. She was eleven years old and had apparently never met the guy. As far as the pirates went, Crudd was one of the cooler ones. But father material? Meh. Lucas's gut wrenched, thinking of fathers. Dad wasn't here rescuing him from the siren like Crudd was for Tabitha. Lucas tried not to be a hypocrite where dads were concerned.

"Crudd—" Captain Flatus jogged over the glass shards past Tabitha to where Crudd dangled by his pinkie finger on the *Scumbucket's* railing. Flatus reached out his hand.

He was a millisecond too late. The sewer siren was back.

"I consulted the sirens, and we accept this trade. This pirate has shown true worth and will become a sentry of Ascaris." Giardia slipped her shadowy fingers around Crudd's last finger clasping the rail. Even though the siren was a whispery ghost-thing, she had plenty strength to pop his hand free. The two of them slipped down into the murk. Only a tiny *plop* serenaded their departure from all things above water.

Lucas was too far away to see them hit the water but remembered his own swan dive all too well. He made an exasperated sound and tiptoed out of and around the minefield of glass.

"Noooo! Man overboard— Man overboard!" Flatus wailed, half hanging over the railing. He reached fruitlessly after Crudd, who'd already plummeted into the depths.

"Flatus—Careful." Lucas finally found a safe path around the glass shards over to the rail and grabbed the captain's boot. He didn't want to lose both Crudd and Flatus in one minute. Despite their lawlessness and poor bodily hygiene, he'd grown fond of the pirates.

Flatus got his bulbous body back on the proper side of the railing, but he wasn't even half-healed from the loss of his crewman. He blubbered like a baby, and tears rinsed the sewer filth from his round red cheeks. Lucas gave him a good-natured whack on the back, but it didn't calm the great oaf's fit.

"Billy Rubin, curse yer mutinous self. Crudd was thrice the pirate you'll ever be," Flatus said.

Lucas suddenly remembered the existence of Billy Rubin. His skin crawled with hatred of him. He grabbed Tabitha's hand and tugged her up to her feet. The threat of the siren was gone for the moment, but the mutinous bugger was still at large.

Tabitha acted like she'd just woken from a disturbing dream. Surprisingly, she kept hold of Lucas's hand.

"You okay? Watch out for the glass," Lucas said. He felt pretty cool for the moment, taking care of the little lady who was typically tougher than Lucas.

"Glass? That's not glass. That's the weapon I gave you, Lucas. I can't believe you broke it already." Her normal demeanor came back quickly. She looked at Lucas's hand and dropped it like it was on fire. Tabitha had majestically transitioned from afraid to mean.

For the first time, Lucas liked it. She was pretty tough to go without a dad her whole life, and a mom at least part of her life, and still be sane. He frowned. Her dad had just shown up and immediately had fallen victim to a siren attack. There was far too much kidnapping from all parties down here in the sewers.

"I'm sorry about your... dad," Lucas said. He wondered if she remembered what had just happened or if she'd been too busy being siren-hypnotized.

"I've never seen him before. He wasn't my dad. Even if he was, he's not anymore." Tabitha's face was stony strong.

Lucas shrugged, at a loss for words.

Tabitha looked down at the water over the railing.

He wasn't anyone's dad anymore.

"I can't find that louse. Billy Rubin is gone," Flatus yelled at the top of his lungs.

The pirate crew scurried around to verify Flatus's statement.

"Gone? Did Giardia get him too?" Lucas asked.

"Gee-arty-who?" Flatus asked.

"Hang on." Simon the big plumber came up behind Lucas and Tabitha.

"Huh?" Lucas looked up at Simon. He had forgotten about him for the moment.

"Hang on." Simon engulfed them both in a big hug from behind that wasn't a second too soon.

Crrunncch. The *Scumbucket* crashed.

"What did we hit?" Flatus muttered.

Lucas opened his eyes but couldn't see Flatus from his position under a pile of bodies, squashed underneath Simon's plump, plumbery self. There was some orange hair in his face which he presumed to be Tabitha's, and Crudd's rat squealed and scratched nearby.

"Villainous, fat-kidneyed, base-born plumbers," Flatus hollered. Plumbers had caused the crash?

"Geddoffamee!" Lucas whined and struggled. It felt like an entire football team was piled on top of him.

"How dare they build this weather-bitten eyesore in me sewer," Flatus carried on.

Simon grunted and rolled off. He kept a grip on Lucas's shoulder and Tabitha's hand as they got their sea-legs back.

"Apparently he don't much like the drainblocker we installed. Nevermind dat. 'Dis way." Simon was scratched up good, probably from the shards of glass spread across the deck. Or the main mast walloping him. Or being stabbed with shanks and slashed with cutlasses. Part of Lucas wondered if Dad was this tough, too. Another part of him was afraid that he wasn't.

All the pirates were strewn about, groaning and moaning about the misfortune of themselves and the *Scumbucket*. Some were bleeding. Some were probably dead.

Lucas shivered and looked up into the darkness as Simon led him and Tabitha through the bodies and the debris on deck. Lucas was too shaken up to ask what was going on, and Tabitha stayed quiet too.

They went away from the poop deck down to the forecastle deck. Lucas had spent time on the poop deck at the ship's stern, but never here at the bow. He laid eyes for the first time on the ship's figurehead, a beautiful mermaid that looked strikingly out of place amongst all the sewer scum. It was reminiscent of the tattoo over Flatus's heart. Flatus's girlfriend? That had to be awkward, with the tail and all. How could they go out to dinner or a movie? Lucas basked in her fishy glory for a moment before Simon snapped him out of it.

"Down here." Simon pointed beyond the figure-head to a little boat tethered in an alcove of the sewer dead-end. There were two dusky figures hunched in the dinghy, shielded with the shadows of the nighttime sewer.

Who was there? Plumbers, maybe? That could be why Simon had led them over, to meet up with the rest of the plumber night-crew. Maybe Dad, too. Lucas had mixed feelings about that. He had a good grounding in store for him when he returned home — he knew that for a fact. But on the upside, Dad wasn't too much of a wuss to come save Lucas. Or at least attempt the rescue.

The *Scumbucket* had crashed into a well-placed metal grate over a smaller chunk of sewer piping where the flow was whitewater-fast. The ship's hull seemed to be holding up against all odds, considering even that shadowy sewer siren had made Swiss cheese out of Flatus's boat. Was this the supposed portal to open sea? Lucas figured the plumbers had installed the grate to catch some of the bigger floaters and chunks of debris. The *Scumbucket* was the prime example of sewer flotsam.

"No, not Matilda," Flatus's voice rang out. He was completely incapable of being quiet.

Lucas turned his head and saw Flatus trample his downed crew as he made a beeline for the bow. Flatus seemed to be worried about the mermaid figurehead. Of all the silly things to be focused on after his pre-cious ship had gotten itself completely owned, it had to be that.

"Matilda, me love," Flatus said.

"It's just a statue, Flatus. Why don't you focus on your ship and your crew, huh?" Lucas rolled his eyes and forgot about manners completely.

"Me one true love—Me Matilda, who I left behind when I got meself—" Flatus stopped his sentence short.

Simon waved down to the dinghy. A grappling hook flew up and hooked itself on the railing. Lucas looked back and forth between Simon and Flatus. Flatus forgot the statue of his lost love. His eyes popped out of his skull with seething hatred. Hatred that could only be against his mortal enemy.

"Plumbers!" Flatus screamed like a Scottish warrior in blue face paint. He hoisted his sharpened towel bar above his head like a battle cry.

"Uh-oh," Lucas said.

"Go! Grab on tight to dat rope and get yer hiney down there," Simon said.

Simon was like a jumbo-sized version of Lucas's dad. He was maybe a bit tougher, and definitely someone Lucas wanted on his side. Lucas was not sure about shimmying down a rope to the tiny sewer dinghy. It looked leagues away and in a dark, creepy, sewer cavern. And without pants.

"Are you sure about this?" Lucas's voice wavered.

"Yeah—Shake a leg, kid," Simon said.

Flatus's crew of pirates forgot their differences and swarmed down around the bow to see what their captain was hollering about. Most of them had recovered their weapons. All of them looked ready to fight.

Another grappling hook flew up and latched onto the bowsprit, dangerously close to the mermaid figurehead. Lucas swallowed. He was sure Flatus would have a fit if his lost love got dislodged and sucked down the sewer pipe they couldn't chase her through. The water roared through the darkness all around them.

Lucas panicked. Should he shimmy his naked bum down the rope attached to the railing? Try to prevent Flatus from exploding like a nuclear bomb?

Simon grew impatient and grabbed onto Tabitha instead. He tried to push her pink pajama-clad body onto the railing, but she planted her feet and shook her head.

"Nuh-uh. I'm not a plumber. I'm a pirate." Tabitha put her hands on her hips.

Lucas smiled at her. She had guts, he'd give her that. Despite watching the father she'd never known meet an untimely demise, she was still tough as nails and planned to support her family via piracy. Maybe it'd work.

"Are you going? Either of you?" Simon asked Lucas and Tabitha. He tapped his big work-boot-clad foot.

A random pirate came up behind Simon. The plumber's fist swung out and met the pirate's flawless smile. The pirate cried and ran off—Simon didn't flinch. Lucas weighed his options. Unfortunately, he weighed them too long.

Viscous Val showed up and hollered a battle cry like the rest of the crew. Nothing like a common enemy to rally the pirates. Val grabbed the grappling hook and ripped it free of the railing. He threw it down into the sewer water, making more noise than Tarzan all the while.

"Hey, you little twerp." Simon grabbed Val's shoulder and gave him a good shake.

"Ha! Whachya gonna do, fatty? Beat up a little kid?" Viscous Val laughed like a hyena.

Simon twitched. He let Val go and punched one fat fist into the palm of his other hand. Lucas wanted him to punch Val but understood why he wouldn't.

"I thought so," Val stuck out his tongue. He turned around and did the little stunt where he farted and pretended to be jet-propelled away. Lucas was not amused, but he still might try the stunt in school tomorrow. It'd be funnier when he did it. That is, if he survived till tomorrow.

"Carl? Lost the grappler up here," Simon called down to the boat.

"Oh snap..." Lucas realized Dad was there. That would make it all the more difficult to stay on as a pirate.

"Clear," Dad's voice shouted from the darkness.

Another grappling hook clunked onto the deck. Simon helped it find a good hold on the railing. He pointed at it and narrowed his eyes at Lucas.

Lucas gulped. The whole stupid point of coming back onto the pirate ship was to save Tabitha. Who didn't actually want to be saved, and was becoming a pirate of her own free will. Maybe it was time to go home.

Lucas looked around for her. Val had his arms wrapped all the way around her pink waist. Lucas's face got hot. A less angry Lucas may have realized that Val was just giving her a boost to free the second grappler from the bowsprit.

"Dad... Ten more minutes?" Lucas had made the same request an innumerable amount of times at home. Ten more minutes playing outside. Ten more minutes before bed. Ten more minutes to wake up.

"Lucas—Take care of him, Simon. Please," Dad yelled.

Lucas scrunched his nose. He hated feeling like he couldn't look after himself. But considering how well he'd taken care of Tabitha, well, maybe his skills could use a little polishing.

Simon knelt down in front of Lucas and laid down the law. "No way, José. We gotta get all these pirates off the ship before we break it up into chunks. Then gotta hoist the fragments up this drain hole with the sewer snakes from the guys above. We can't just let this hunk o' junk ship clog the city's sewer forever."

"Hunk o' junk? The *Scumbucket* is me life, and ye will have to sink me before ye sink her." Flatus burst onto the scene. He was the poster child for insanity, tangled blond hair flying out behind him and crazy eyes set deeply in his red face. He swung his cutlass with more finesse than Lucas had given him credit for.

"You asked for it." Simon whistled, a long shrill sound that reverberated off the sewer walls, time and time again.

Lucas resisted the urge to plug his ears. He didn't want to appear weaker than he already had, half-naked and dirty. Someone pushed past him roughly and ran for the railing at light speed.

"Billy?" Flatus's attention shifted from the plumber to the mutineer.

Billy Rubin shed his coat and buckled boots on the deck before he launched himself over the railing. Against all odds, he grabbed onto the grappling hook's rope and clung there like a monkey. He started scooting down toward the plumbers' dinghy.

"That's not Lucas," Dad's voice yelled from down below.

"Who is it, then?" another plumber asked in the dark.

"Sanctuary! Sanctuary," Billy Rubin squealed and scooted down the rope that had been intended for Lucas.

"Hey—" Lucas tried to grab him before he went overboard, but was too late. He grabbed the discarded pirate coat and yanked the frilly thing over his pillow-case garb, despite himself. His sore feet found relief and sanctuary of their own in Billy's silly boots. Lucas didn't care a bit how ridiculous he sounded, clopping over the deck like a horse.

"Cut the rope," Simon said.

"Aye-aye," said Flatus.

For once, the pirates and the plumbers agreed on something. Flatus used his blade to shred the thick rope in a few whacks. Billy begged for mercy, but his whining was cut off with the rope he clung to.

"Aiiiieeeee," Billy yelped before the *sploosh* notified everyone of his exit from the *Scumbucket*. He had joined his true kin, the sludgy, slimy, sewer scum. Good riddance.

"Huzzah!" Everyone cheered.

For a moment, just a split second really, everything seemed like it was working out all right. Then the kraken grabbed Flatus Codswallup around the middle and hoisted him into the air.

Chapter Ten

"Yarrr. Lemme go, lubbers. Get yer kraken off me," Flatus kicked as he hovered over the *Scumbucket's* deck in the grasp of the sewer snake.

Simon whistled again through his moustache. Lucas plugged his ears and dodged Flatus's kicking feet. The so-called kraken dropped Flatus unceremoniously. He didn't have much to say about it as the writhing mechanical tentacle moved on to its proper target. The mizzen mast. Had the second tallest mast been promoted to main mast now that the main mast was no more than a floating log? Lucas wasn't sure but decided it didn't matter. The mizzen mast was about to meet its maker, too.

"No! Not me precious *Scumbucket*," Flatus wailed and picked himself up off the deck.

The rest of his pirate crew waited, weapons at the ready, for some sense of what to do. They hadn't had the best luck fighting the kraken last time, as the missing main mast proudly declared. And Flatus's begging didn't seem to be helping much either. The sewer snake started wailing on the mizzenmast and a fine snow of toilet-paper sail shreds fell over the deck. Lucas sputtered as he inhaled some of the TP dandruff.

Another grappling hook latched onto the *Scumbucket's* railing. And another.

Lucas wasn't sure what he'd say to Dad if he boarded the ship. Nothing reasonable, in all likelihood. He felt for Flatus though, and hoped some sort of truce could be reached.

Flatus ran toward the mizzen and busted out his blunderbuss. He shot it up at the kraken and missed horribly. His portable grappling hook reeled itself in as Flatus started a new plan of defense.

"Crew—Got us a plan. Ye, ye, and ye, climb up the rigging an' free the mizzen from the kraken's grasp. Ye lot o'er there, get below deck an' man the cannons. Crudd, get the lantern on those plumbers down—" Flatus stopped abruptly.

Lucas could feel the sorrow in his voice. The captain had forgotten Crudd was no longer among his crew. Flatus still wanted to rely on him. He was needed now, but no. That was all said and done. The siren had taken him.

The rest of the pirates scampered off to do what they were told, except Crudd. He was history.

Lucas frowned. He felt a bit torn; he'd almost gone willingly with Giardia. What would have become of him if he had followed through? Would he have become some weird siren-guard-thing like Crudd? Or was that a lie? Maybe they ate pirate meat down in Ascaris.

Lucas wondered if there was any chance Crudd could survive it. Either way, he'd probably never be seen again. Poor luck, Crudd had. That was the risk of being a good dude. Save your own skin, or save a girl in peril. He'd saved her, not himself. His daughter. Lucas felt downright gloomy.

Simon whistled again. The kraken responded—it let the shredded sail go and clamped onto the mast itself. The ship jolted, and the mechanical tentacle grew taut. Lucas watched, frozen in horror of the *Scumbucket's* demise.

Someone grabbed Lucas from behind. He screamed like a girl.

"Dingleberry—It's me. It's Dad. I've got you." Dad's unmistakable voice found Lucas's ear.

Dad had crept up behind Lucas undetected during all the commotion. He'd clamped his hand over Lucas's mouth and silenced his shriek before it left his throat. His hand smelled like bleach and drain declogger, a shocking difference from the stench of poo. Lucas still tried to pry his hand off and get a word in. Dad was stronger than he looked and lifted him clean off the deck. He bounced on Dad's belly as he struggled to be set back on his own two feet.

"Don't worry, Lucas, I'm taking you home. Come on."

If not for the *Scumbucket's* predicament, Lucas would have left happily with Dad, skipping through the goo and up the sewer drain, back home to a hot shower. But things had gotten messy. Maybe he wasn't really part of the crew just yet; he had never signed anything or made any agreements, but he still cared what happened to them all. He wasn't going to let all these pirates end up homeless hobos, even though they were already dressing the part.

Lucas squirmed and tried to escape, or at least free his mouth to plead his case. He had no such luck. Dad dragged him toward the set of grappling hooks looped over the *Scumbucket's* railing. He dropped Lucas and pointed down to the jollyboat. He wore his plumber uniform, dorky hat and all, and matched whoever was down in the boat below. The boat plumber waved up at them. Were there two people in the boat? Lucas couldn't be sure through the murk.

"Time to go," Dad said.

Lucas finally had freedom to talk and walk, but the confused knot in his stomach made him stumble over what he wanted to express. Lucas took the first few steps toward the railing but then paused. Maybe he could just go, follow an order from Dad for once, be home safe—No. He really couldn't.

"No, This is insanity." Lucas flailed his arms around and struggled to express what he knew in his heart was wrong.

"Yeah, I know, Dingleberry. You running off to become a pirate in the middle of the night without any pants on? Pure insanity. You scared me really bad when you jumped in that manhole. Why'd you do it? Care about pirates more than your dear old dad? I'm taking you home. You're not getting another chance to wind up dead tonight, Lucas. The rest of the guys will finish up here." He pointed at the ropes again.

Unfortunately for Dad, at that moment, the cannons fired. *Kabooommm.* The bulky ship swayed back and forth. The plumbers' ropes were vaporized. Lucas saw the severed grappling hooks with their little frayed stubs of singed rope as the smoke cleared. His ears rang and stung, but his heart lightened. Flatus's pirates weren't going extinct today.

"No!" Dad yelled.

Simon whistled, but the sewer snake couldn't respond properly anymore. One of the pirates had climbed the riggings and cut off its grasping-claw end. Surprisingly, sewer shanks and plunger cutlasses were tougher than plumber snakes. Sweet. It flailed around like a dying earthworm on a fishhook. Simon shot Dad a look and shrugged hopelessly.

"We had a truce, plumber," Flatus Codswallup roared. He marched over and stuck his finger into Dad's chest.

"You broke it when you took my son." Dad's eyes looked wet and threatened to tear.

Lucas looked on in awe. He wasn't sure who to root for. He didn't want either of them to die tonight, and a truce seemed unlikely. He gulped.

"Puke here didn't flush. Ye well know that be how we hone in on potential recruits fer the crew." Flatus waved his fat gun around.

"Yes, he did. I specifically warned him to flush so your filthy lot of pirates wouldn't come into our house," Dad argued.

Lucas looked sheepishly at him. Should he re-mind him about today during dinner? He swallowed hard.

"Uh, Dad?"

"I specifically... I specifically warned you." A vein bulged on Dad's neck. He looked at Lucas, then back to Flatus, then back to Lucas. The looks on their faces said it all. Dad knew that Lucas had failed him. The look of betrayal, of being let down by his only son, broadcasted across his face.

Lucas's mouth went dry, and he was ashamed. Fighting for the wrong side.

"I'm—I'm sorry," Lucas shrugged helplessly.

Some pirates came up behind Simon and Carl and cuffed their hands together with shower curtain rings.

Lucas reached out toward Dad. "No!" he yelled.

"Yes," Flatus argued. He reached down and whacked Lucas on the back.

Lucas bit his tongue. "What are you going to do with them?" He was afraid to know the answer. He wiped some blood off his mouth with his ruffled sleeve. He cringed, knowing where it had been.

"That coat looks mighty snappy on yerself, Puke. Glad Billy Rubin had the wits to leave it behind when he fled fer his life." Flatus laughed.

"Flatus? What are you going to do with the plumbers?" Lucas begged to know.

"Why, we be going to hang 'em, o' course." Flatus looked downright jolly.

"No!" Lucas was a bit obnoxious with uninvited yelps and shouts. He could recall screaming something contrary at least a dozen times this evening. But he really couldn't help it this time. There was no way he'd stand silent while Dad got hung on the *Scumbucket*, deep down in the sewer. Swinging to death with a rope around his neck, in this dark dank place. What a crappy way to die—pun intended.

"What, Puke? No stomach for a good hanging?" Viscous Val jabbed him hard in the ribs with an elbow.

"Shut up. How can you be so wicked?" Tabitha snapped and wedged her way between him and Lucas.

Lucas grinned, forgetting for a split-second why he was somber. It was nice having Tabitha on his side. She would be a pretty hardcore friend. Not many guys would want this pint-sized fiery redhead at their throats.

One of the pirates passed around a small keg of grog, reeking of strong peppermint. Everyone sucked a mouthful right out of the barrel and gargled loudly. There was no way Lucas was going to gargle grog this time, even if he had turds stuck between his teeth. This was no time to celebrate. He shoved the keg away from him when it got passed his direction.

"This is wrong." Lucas looked around for Flatus. Only the pirate captain could stop this, and he'd probably need some convincing. What could he say? How had a person stopped a hanging back in the dark ages when they did that primeval stuff?

"Don't worry, they can't go through with it. They can't possibly hang them." Tabitha speculated.

Lucas nodded and puffed himself up with resolve. He would stop this. He would stop this now.

"Flatus!" Lucas screamed as loud as his lungs could handle.

"Address Cap'n properly, Puke." Chummy said.

He'd appeared out of nowhere just to chide Lucas. Yuck. His puckered pruney face was full of judgment. And all Lucas thought of when he saw the wrinkled, old, one-eyed Chummy was how he'd supported Billy Rubin in the absence of Flatus. What a jerk. Normally he'd say something obnoxious in retort, but was distracted at the moment.

"Where is he?" Lucas asked.

"He's very busy right now, preparing for—" Chummy started.

"Where. Is. He." Lucas spat the words like a venomous snake.

"He be... in his cabin, Puke. Waiting till we be done preparing the hanging." Chummy seemed shaken by the ferocity of Lucas's voice.

Good.

He shoved the makeshift first mate in the shoulder and sprinted toward the captain's door marked *W.C.* In spite of everything, Lucas still thought that was a stupid thing to write on a door. *Where's Cap'n?* Ha. He tried the knob, but it was latched on the inside. He pounded on it and peered through the moon-shaped cutout.

"Flatus—Let me in. We need to talk. Now," Lucas spoke faster than he was used to.

"Calm down, be professional and respectful, and maybe he'll listen to you." Tabitha appeared at his elbow.

Lucas looked at her, started to get annoyed, then changed his mind. He nodded. She was right, and he needed to practice not hating her. He'd try. Especially if they both lost their dads today… he better not hate her. She better not make him hate her. He'd need someone to complain to.

"Don't get yer britches in a bunch, Dingleberry," Flatus said.

Flatus walked over noisily and unlatched the door. He regarded the two kids at his doorstep for a moment before ushering them inside.

"Don't call me that. Only Dad gets to call me that." Lucas growled.

"Aye-aye," Flatus said.

"You can't possibly hang them. Are you really that heartless?" Tabitha piped up.

Lucas liked that she dropped the formal pirate salutations. Flatus had ceased to deserve respect in his eyes.

"Heartless?" Flatus looked amused.

"You think this is funny? I told you I didn't want to be a part of your stupid stinky crew. I told you I didn't want to stay. I told you I wanted to go home. I know why now. You're vicious. You're monsters," Lucas ranted and raved.

"Hurts me heart t'hear that from ye, Puke. I had such high hopes fer ye as a recruit," Flatus mused.

"Never. *Never*. I am not on your crew. I'll never be a stinky, sewer-sailing privyteer or a rancid, outhouse pirate. I'm going to grow up and become a plumber, just to fight you," Lucas carried on.

"I'll be resigning from your crew too, if you actually hang them," Tabitha said.

Lucas admired her tact.

"Jus' like yer dads. Both of ye," Flatus said.

Flatus looked back and forth between them. His eyes darkened and lowered.

Tabitha made a sound that Lucas couldn't decipher. Maybe a stifled sob. Maybe a deleted remark.

"Aye. It be clear to me now what yer problem be," Flatus said.

Lucas paused and looked at the pirate captain. He didn't look evil. He was deceiving. He acted ridiculous and silly and smelled like he bathed in sewer water, but inside he was pure evil. Lucas ground his teeth together.

"I know what yer beef with me be now, Puke, and I have the perfect solution fer all of us. 'Cept mayhaps me. It doesn't sit quite right with me, not yet, anyhow…" Flatus paced across his cabin.

"What's your solution, then?" Tabitha asked.

"You'll all hang together," Flatus said.

Lucas wasn't sure how he'd managed to get their situation from bad to worse. All four were now tied up. Dad, Lucas, Tabitha, and Simon. The pirates had bound their hands behind their backs with shower curtain rings and lashed their feet together with over-sized sticky bandages. They'd been blindfolded with damp rags, and Lucas had to rely on sound and smell to perceive what was going on.

It seemed like a proper party for the pirates. Minty splashes of grog were spat all over the deck and shouts of *huzzah* rang out every couple minutes. Lucas realized he could never have been happy as a pirate. For every cool thing, like a Jolly Plunger, there was an opposite dark thing, like a hanging. He ground his teeth together helplessly.

"Don't worry, Dingleberry. Things will work out," Dad whispered toward Lucas's ear.

Lucas opened his mouth to respond, but all that came out was a big sob. He snapped it shut. He didn't want to be a weakling in front of all these people. Especially in his last moments of existence. But it was too late. His body shook with big shaking bursts of tears that started in his gut and poured out his eyes, soaking the blindfold.

"Ha, Puke's crying. Whaaaa," Viscous Val teased from the crowd.

Someone spit a big mouthful of minty grog at the prisoners, splashing Lucas's bare feet. He cringed and tried to back up. He squeezed into the group of bound prisoners, but there wasn't anywhere to escape.

Tabitha felt a bit shaky at his side, but for some reason, neither of the plumbers seemed concerned. They stood there quietly, waiting for their fate. Maybe that's what adulthood was, just waiting to die. Maybe only the kids had something to live for. Lucas didn't like that thought, but he was too confused and upset to make another hypothesis.

Some stinky pirate with minty fresh breath moved around the group. Lucas gulped, trying to stifle his tears. He didn't want to die a coward. It was too late to make a difference. He had no free hands to grab, no free legs to kick, and he doubted anyone was stupid enough to get within biting range.

"Ah!" Tabitha squeaked.

"Are you okay?" Lucas asked her.

That was a stupid question. Pathetically stupid. Even if he didn't die a coward, he was going to die an idiot. Who asks someone if they're okay while being hanged to death?

"This rat won't get off me. It's climbing up my... eeek! It tickles," Tabitha squealed again.

"There's worse things than rats." Like being hanged.

Someone looped a chunk of rope around his middle and cinched it up tight. He tried to calm his racing heart, breathing slowly, deeply. He thought the rope was supposed to be around his neck, but didn't want to correct whoever was placing it. Especially if he was doing it wrong... That was a good thing.

"I be sorry t'see ye go, Puke. Ye would have made a fine recruit. Ye too, little Cruddlet. We'll all be sorry t'see ye both go." Flatus's voice was unmistakable.

Lucas gathered up some spit and tried his best to aim it at the sound of the captain's voice. *Hurrkk... ptooie.* A couple pirates laughed, but it hadn't seemed to hit home. He sighed and hoped it'd be over quickly.

"Clamp them with the kraken," Chummy said.

Lucas was still thoroughly annoyed that Chummy, who'd been all ready to support the mutinous Billy Rubin, had brownnosed himself into the first mate position. There was plenty more to be annoyed with at the moment, though, so Lucas tried to let it go. The guy was about a hundred years old anyway; his service wouldn't be long even if Flatus had promoted him.

There was some movement on the deck, heavy footsteps and a *thunk* that sounded like the plunger peg-leg.

The rope around their midsections tightened up. It didn't feel like a rope at all, really. It felt like a garden hose. The sewer snake? They were getting bound up with that thing? Lucas hated being blind and dumb to the happenings. He held his breath.

"Hang em up," Flatus roared.

"Aye-aye, Cap'n," Chummy's phlegmy voice answered.

Simon's ear-piercing whistle split the rank air.

That was the last time Lucas's feet touched the deck of the *Scumbucket*.

Chapter Eleven

Lucas hadn't realized he wasn't being killed until they'd been yanked halfway up the pipe. They followed the path of the sewer snake as it recoiled in response to Simon's whistle.

Lucas was pretty sure he'd peed himself but couldn't really tell among the dampness and smells of the sewer anyway. The rest of the plumber crew at the other end of the kraken hauled them up and hosed them off before sending them on their way home.

Tabitha had probably been the calmest of the entire bunch, though sad about her failed attempt at piracy. She'd somberly waved goodbye when they dropped her off at Granny's house. Crudd's rat was still with her and hadn't left her side for an instant.

When Dad and Lucas got home, everything seemed way too normal. Chelsea bragged to her brother that she had been creative and climbed up into the kitchen sink to go potty. Desperate times had called for desperate measures, and Lucas had locked her out of the bathroom all night instead of the few minutes he'd intended. Lucas gave her a high five for her inventiveness, but all she did was cry over his high five being too hard. Lucas rolled his eyes but was still seriously glad to see her again.

Mom had decided to follow up the dance aerobics with yoga, and was deep into it when Dad and Lucas showed up, smelling of the sewer.

"Shower — now," Mom hollered and switched off the TV.

"No prob-lem-o. And by the way, Mom, thanks for the swimming lessons." Lucas had remembered his pledge to be grateful, for once.

Mom looked confused but still smiled before shooing them toward the bathroom.

The only thing better than being alive was taking a hot shower. Lucas let Dad go first. That was about the nicest thing he'd ever done, and the warm look on Dad's face showed he appreciated the respect. When it was Lucas's turn, he used up all the hot water. Every last drop.

The next day at school, Tabitha looked the same as always. Lucas's stomach rolled with anxiety, but he took his seat next to her anyway.

"Granny was stuck in the toilet when I got home because somebody stole the seat." Tabitha growled.

"Who would do such a thing?" Lucas feigned innocence. They both knew full-well who had done such a thing.

"Let me think…" She shot him another mean look, but it fizzled into laughter quickly. There were worse fates than broken toilets.

"What'd you do with the rat?" Lucas asked.

"I told Granny it's a hamster."

"At least you have something to remember your, uh, Crudd."

"Whatever. I never had a dad. Granny and I are just fine. We always have been. But at least now I have a hamster."

"Hey, um, can I call you Tab now? Or do you hate me?" Lucas asked.

"Yeah, I guess. Call me Tab. I'm kinda bored with hating you at this point," Tab said.

One surprising consequence of Lucas's sewer adventure was the improvement in his flushing habits. He still enjoyed his toilet time as much as anyone, but he was also happy to flush and wave the mess goodbye. He imagined dropping little stinky hailstones on the deck of the *Scumbucket*.

He couldn't forgive Flatus for making him believe he was going to die, alongside Dad and Tab. That was just wrong. Even when the captain was being nice, he was a complete doofus. He did not want to be flushed again, ever. The risk of being siren-napped and dragged into the depths also lurked at the back of his mind. Crudd would never have a proper burial. No one would ever know, for sure, what had happened to him. A fate worse than death. He shuddered.

Lucas managed to keep up with the toilet-flushing habit for about a month before there was a water conservation presentation at school. He had no clue it took two gallons of water for each flush of the toilet. If he had, he'd have rubbed it in the face of his parents long ago for forcing him to be so wasteful with the flushing.

"If it's yellow, let it mellow," Lucas preached to his family. He was quick to convert to environmentalist mode.

"Lucas..." Dad stared at him meaningfully.

"What? If it's brown, flush it down," Lucas finished.

"No. That's filthy. You'll flush no matter what color it is. I see enough bodily waste at work. No need to see it in my own toilet." Dad ended the conversation.

Lucas knew the truth, even if Dad hadn't been willing to say it outright in front of Mom and Chelsea. Dad was trying to prevent pirate invasions. Bathroom kidnappings. Lucas gave up for the time being. It wasn't worth the fight.

But one night, after the memories of the ordeal on the *Scumbucket* faded with time, when he was the last to use the toilet before bed... he skipped the flush.

"Let it mellow. I'm saving the world. Preserving drinking water." Lucas's dreams had been filled with all sorts of environmental heroics before Chelsea's high-pitched shrieking woke him up way too early on a Saturday morning.

"Lucas? What did you put in the toilet?" Chelsea automatically blamed her brother when he staggered in like a morning zombie.

"It's just pee. I just let it mellow—" Lucas shut up when he saw it too.

There was a corked, brown bottle in the toilet bowl. It bobbed like a legit buoy. Lucas grabbed it out without a thought of bacteria infestation. Urine was sterile, Mrs. Anthony had told him so. And besides, this was surgeon-sterile compared to the sewer system.

The bottle was old-fashioned and weathered. There was a note rolled up inside, safe and dry underneath the cork. Lucas unplugged it and was greeted with a stale puff of sewer-scented air. Memories flooded back. The paper was thick and lumpy, maybe an ancient parchment, or maybe some sewer-soaked toilet paper dried into a fake, old document.

"I'm telling Mom that you put garbage in the toilet." Chelsea ran off squealing into their parents' room.

Lucas unfurled the paper and read it.

Dear Puke the Dingleberry,

On behalf o' the crew o' the newly renovated and re-built Scumbucket *and her Captain Flatus Codswallup, ye be hereby invited for a contractual pirate job at yer earliest convenience. The sewer-siren threat has tripled an' new recruits be necessary. Please RSVP by flushing yer response in this here bottle. An' bring grog.*

Sincerely,
Captain Flatus Codswallup

The bottom of the paper had two flaps, one with the word *Aye* and one with the word *Nay*.

Lucas couldn't say yes. No, never. They were filthy and rude and scared him. They'd let Tab's dad fall to his doom. Even if there was some secret siren sanctuary underneath the murky alligator infested sewer water... Ascaris, the siren had called it.

Giardia. Such a pretty name the siren had. Maybe this was Lucas's one chance to quench his curiosity about the siren town and be a good dude at the same time. He ripped off the *Nay* and examined it. His last chance.

Seconds ticked by, and he rubbed his finger over the parchment. He heard the sounds of Dad grumbling as Chelsea drug him toward the bathroom. Dad would never stand for this. He only had a couple seconds left to decide...

Lucas crumpled up the *Nay* and threw it in the wastebasket.

"If it's brown, flush it down." Lucas left the *Aye* dangling on the notice, jammed it back in the bottle, and recorked it. He pulled the flusher and sent the brown glass bottle down to the *Scumbucket*.

About the Author

J.J. Zbylski is a pharmacist by day, author by night, and a full-time pirate at heart. As a member of American Mensa, The DREAD Fleet, and Absolute Write, J.J. keeps active in her community. J.J. lives in Phoenix, Arizona with the best landlubber family any pirate could wish for.